Pursued by the Crooked Man

SUSAN TROTT

Pursued by the Crooked Man

a novel

1817

HARPER & ROW, PUBLISHERS   New York
Cambridge, Philadelphia, San Francisco, Washington
London, Mexico City, São Paulo,
Singapore, Sydney

FIRST EDITION

Designer: Ruth Bornschlegel

Copy editor: Marjorie Horvitz

Library of Congress Cataloging-in-Publication Data
Trott, Susan.
Pursued by the crooked man.
I. Title.
PS3570.R594P87   1988   813'.54   87-12112
ISBN 0-06-015853-0

---

88 89 90 91 92 HC 10 9 8 7 6 5 4 3 2 1

to Sam

This story is also dedicated to the great Dizzy Gillespie, who took me to lunch when I was a teenager (thirty years ago!) and made a big impression. I told him I wanted to be a writer and he told me how he became a musician. Do you remember, Dizzy, wherever you are?

*Inexpressible thanks to
Jonathan Dolger and Hugh Van Dusen,
who believed*

"Rhyme drugs and stupefies the poignancy of feeling that otherwise could not be borne."

Wordsworth, by way of Powys

PART I

one

*M*iliana Bartha *always believed* her life would end in murder. "I am the sort of person," she would say, "who, when she is found garroted, knifed, or shot, will have, among her acquaintance, none who is above suspicion. It is not that I am surrounded by enemies but that I am a troublemaker. Everyone I know and love has wanted to kill me at some point, and I can't say that I blame them."

"Sure, Mom," her son, Adam, was apt to scoff, because it is hard for young children to see their parents in such interesting terms as troublemakers. However, as he grew older—he was now eighteen—he began to get an inkling that this might in fact be true. She was not like other mothers. Not at all. Still, it was his duty to scoff at Miliana's verbal extravagances, and she actually encouraged him in this. Not for the world would she have him worry about, or fear, this inevitable death of hers by violence.

On this mild morning in late February, in her small, pleasant house, preparing to go down on her knees to scrub the kitchen floor, Miliana was thinking about death and what, besides her children, she would leave the world in the event of it. What legacy?

Even on a dazzling day such as this one, plangent with birdsong, such gloomy thoughts can be pardoned and understood, thought Miliana, by anyone who ever has had to go down on her knees to scrub.

3

But the truth was that she felt so strangely weary that thoughts of inexorable sickness were seeping into her mind, and the idea of death by murder seemed comparatively delightful and liberating.

But no, she assured herself, I am not ailing, I am only spoiled because it's been so many years since I've had to scrub a kitchen floor.

Recently, after a stern look at her finances, she had determined on an economic retreat and begun it by relinquishing her cleaning lady, Mrs. Fisk.

And I'm not as young as I was. "I am not now that which I have been," as Byron put it. I have only to look in the mirror and see, as I did for the first time yesterday, that the laugh lines from my eyes have met and embraced the laugh lines from my smiles. The dreaded crosshatching has begun. Yes, there has been a meeting of wrinkles, a grand assembly, a wrinkles summit.

Maximiliana—Miliana to her friends, Max to her lovers, Mom to her kids—set down the yellow bucket containing a pungent and vaporous mixture of powders and fluids. She had thrown in everything under the kitchen sink, feeling that the more soil removers in the bucket, the less elbow grease beyond the bucket. In fact, it seemed to her the aroma alone should scour the floor. She wasn't sure that the cleansers were compatible, for the mixture seemed to be roiling and hissing in alarmed emulsibility. She drew on a pair of rubber gloves so as not to mutilate her hands, and assumed the prehistorical position.

She was a first-generation Argentinian and, as an expatriate, also a last-generation Argentinian, daughter of a Hungarian father and a Czechoslovakian mother, both Jews. Her children were native Americans, and the U.S.A. was the country of her soul. Her two husbands were first-generation North Americans. The children's father, Jones, was of German-Canadian descent, while her second husband, Dominic Racatelli, from whom she had fled six years before and from whom she was still in hiding, was of Sicilian-Sicilian.

Miliana was a tall, stunning woman with fair hair, enhanced weekly, dark heavy-lidded eyes, a thin, beaked nose, and full lips that smiled even while she slept.

A stranger meeting her now would think that she must have been extraordinarily beautiful when young, but in fact she'd got better-looking every year.

As she commenced her scrub, her Gioconda lips were the channel for an amorphous singsong sound that seemingly, at first, had nothing to do with her inevitable death by violence and subsequent lack of legacy: "Georgie Porgie, puddin' and pie, kissed the girls and made them cry."

She had raised her children on Mother Goose nursery rhymes and for some reason the verses were flooding back to her consciousness and getting a clawlike grip on her mind—a webbed claw, she presumed.

Maybe, she thought, it is because this is the first time I have gone down on all fours to scrub since the children were babies, and there is something about my physical posture and the scrubbing motion that has unlocked these rhymes from my mind and sent them all surging back to me. How interesting!

"Georgie Porgie, puddin' and pie . . . How I always detested Georgie. Whereas Tom, Tom, the baker's man, was a prince."

She sat back on her heels and dropped the rag into the bucket. She tilted her head upward, listening. It was as if God Himself, or Mother Goose Herself, were speaking to her, saying, This is it! Do it!

5

"I beg your pardon?"—head still tilted. "Do what?"
Tell the world!

Very well, she thought, resuming her task. I will tell the world, if the world is waiting to hear, how I detested Georgie Porgie and what a crumb I always thought he was.

She laughed at the idea of the world being on tenterhooks to hear this, but she believed there was something to it—to this "Do it!" Something was happening here that could not be denied.

I must tell the world, she realized, my feelings about *all* the nursery rhymes. I must penetrate to the heart of their mysteries so that they are not mere babble and in so doing explain what Mother Goose *meant.* This will be my legacy!

But first I will finish the floor. One must take these things in order.

With her weight on both knees and one hand, she backed across the beige tiles, the other hand bearing down and moving in a sweeping motion. She was excited about the task that lay ahead of her, as who would not be. It is so exhilarating to be *selected,* as it definitely seemed to her she'd been. As well, she had felt purposeless of late, inconsequential. It had been a long while since she'd caused any trouble.

But this, she thought, won't create trouble, but art. It will be a contribution.

I feel quite as Abraham must have after God said to take his son, Isaac, to the land of Moriah and make of him a burnt offering on one of the mountains of that place— which mountain he would tell Abraham when he got there. At last, after a hundred and ten years, Abraham had someplace to go and something to do.

Of course, my job will be harder. God was just fooling around with Abraham, who was a great favorite of his, virtually giving him a vacation in the guise of having to go and sacrifice his only beloved son, the main seed of a great nation of Jews, whereas I have a serious job at hand here—to make sense of nonsense.

There will be a series of essays, she saw, each one interpreting a rhyme, or perhaps a set of rhymes. I will be the channel for Mother Goose's true intentions but also will not quail to express my own enthusiasms and prejudices.

I wonder if Mother Goose has ever appeared to anyone before?

By now the voice had assumed the proportions of an appearance. Mother Goose had become manifest to Miliana in her kitchen.

I really feel quite puffed up about the whole thing, she thought. She did. She felt energized. Her strange weariness had dissipated.

She saw feet appear on the hardwood floor beyond. She could tell without raising her head, by the Top-Siders, no socks, and khaki pant cuffs, that it was her son, Adam. Were it her lover Tom Flynn, she would see Top-Siders, socks, and jeans. If it were her lover Joel Jarnding, work boots and corduroys.

But Tom and Joel always called before arriving at her house. All of her friends were strictly enjoined to call first. They did not know why it was so important to Miliana, but the reason for this was that she did not wish to be surprised by any appearance—except of her children from college or of Mother Goose from the ether. She was always on her guard for the reappearance in her life of her second (and actually current) husband, Dominic Racatelli, who was pursuing her to the death. He would not stop until he found her, and when he did . . . In her mind she drew a finger across her throat. Dominic was unique among her friends in that he had not wanted to kill her "at some point" in their relationship: he had wanted to kill her for years.

But he had not found her and he would not find her, because she would not relax her guard. She had outwitted him so far, and if by some miracle he did appear, this house had many exits and her mind had laid down many escape routes beyond the exits. At any moment she could disappear without a trace, leaving no spoor. She had done as much before. She could scent him from afar. She had a powerful sixth sense.

Meanwhile, "Hi, Mom."

"Hi, sweetheart." She sat back on her haunches and smiled at the blond, blue-eyed, astonishing handsomeness of her only beloved son, who attended the University of California at Berkeley, known, in the obsessive American way of giving soubriquets to everything, even colleges, as Cal. "Don't step on the floor."

"Why are you doing that?" He sounded truly concerned. He had reached the age at which a son does not like to see his mother scrubbing floors, because it might reflect badly on himself should his friends hear of it. Fifteen years before, he would simply have played cars in the wake of her passage across the tiles, and fifteen years thence it would sincerely give him pain for her sake to find his old mother on her knees, scrubbing, but now, at eighteen, he felt embarrassed and annoyed—which is to say truly concerned for himself. "Where's Mrs. Fisk?" he demanded querulously.

"To answer your first question, I am washing the floor

because it is a time-honored method for removing dirt. As for Mrs. Fish, she's no longer with us. I have given her up. I am saving money. It's funny we never speak of laying off help. Instead we 'give them up.' It makes us spoiled women sound noble and sacrificial." She stood easily, not having to push off with her hands, which she noted that Adam noted. She stripped off her gloves and gave Adam a hug and kiss. "Are you home for the weekend?" she asked. He said that he was. "Good. I have something I want you to read, but first I have to write it, and before that I have to think about what it is I'm going to write. Still, it's bound to be done while you are here. It is clamoring to be set down. It will be the first part of my legacy." Joyfully, she told him about Mother Goose. "Adam, I'm so excited."

"Why not begin right now?" he encouraged her. "I want to go for a run on the mountain, so I'll be gone a couple of hours."

This child of her womb, one of her three main seeds, was a promising runner as well as smart and handsome. All this should have made him insufferably arrogant, but his arrogance was surprisingly sufferable, at least to her, but then she was his mother. She wondered if his friends suffered it as well as she did.

He uncovered his long, lean, elegant body, put on white running shorts and shoes. She followed him out the door to watch his efficient, easy, high-stepping stride take him down the road to where the trails began, then she let her own slow, sensual stride take her back into the house.

Through the big view window she saw the fog from the ocean feeling its way over the greening hills. Her house and the mountain behind were still in sun and, since she'd learned every vagary of this coastal fog, she knew it would stay sunny and Adam would have a warm, dry run. How she loved that boy. How lucky she was, how rich her life. And now she was handed this wonderful creative task, to enrich and enlighten her existence even more. She often wondered why it was given to her to have such a lovely time on this planet while so much of the world suffered. But she never felt guilty; she just felt lucky.

Certainly life had been difficult at times, but she had never once been bored.

One thing about being pursued, she thought, is that it keeps you young and on your toes. There's no putting your feet up for very long, no throwing in the sponge.

The kitchen tiles were still gleaming with wetness. She was tempted to cross to the refrigerator for a glass of wine but abandoned the idea and instead went directly to her drop-leaf fruitwood table and pulled up one of the leaves. She set out a yellow pad of paper and a black fine-point pen. She pulled up a chair and placed it before the table. But still she didn't sit down. One doesn't embark on a legacy so easily. It's not like sitting down and writing a letter. It is not a lark.

She wandered around her living room, ran her fingers over the keys of the upright piano, adjusted a few books in the shelves so the bindings were aligned, put fresh water in her vase of yellow roses, stacked the magazines on the coffee table, straightened one of the Oriental rugs, which like the books were worn and faded with use and therefore more luminous.

All this time her mind was forming words and images, and now, in almost a trancelike state, she drifted to the chair and sat down. In a loose, flowing hand, she wrote her first interpretive piece for Mother Goose. Adam returned from his run, and still she wrote. Adam showered, lunched, made phone calls, stretched out on the couch and read *The Great Gatsby* halfway through, while Miliana wrote on. Adam left the house to visit with a friend, and when he returned it was early evening. Then it was that Miliana put down her pen, stood up creakily, walked a few awkward steps. Gone for the nonce her sensual stride, her smiling lips. She was stiff and sore. It was a new experience to sit in one place for so long. She handed the pages to Adam, who read aloud the title: "Mother Goose Nursery Rhymes and What on Earth They Mean," and declared it cumbersome.

"Never mind," said Miliana. "Read on."

"Do you know that this is the first time in my life I ever saw you *do* anything?"

"Never mind."

"In fact, you did two things today: washed the floor and wrote this essay. It's unprecedented."

Adam started to read, spurred on by the feeling that he was at last going to find something out about his mother.

The rhyme about Georgie Porgie is not too hard to understand. "Georgie Porgie, pudding and pie, / Kissed the girls and made them cry. / When the boys came out to play, / Georgie Porgie ran away."

Georgie Porgie is a loathsome character. He's a bully. He makes the girls cry, but then, when the boys come out, he cravenly runs away for fear they'll hit him.

Why did the girls cry? Because Georgie Porgie *forced* his kisses on them and it was intolerable to be kissed by him. He wasn't bad-looking, but he was such a *worm*.

When the boys, who had been studying (something

the undisciplined and stupid Georgie never did), came out to play, they were stunned to see all the girls in tears, but when they saw Georgie Porgie running away—which he always did whenever the boys appeared—then they knew the girls were crying because Georgie Porgie had been forcing his vile kisses upon them once again.

As usual, the boys did nothing about it. You know this has happened before and will happen again. Over and over again. It's a nightmare for the girls.

Moving on to Tom, Tom, the baker's man, we find a rhyme that is a hard nut to crack. "Tom, Tom, the baker's man, / Stole a pig and away he ran; / The pig was eat, / And Tom was beat, / And Tom ran crying down the street."

It breaks my heart to limn the lines. Why should Tom, of all people, be beat, and made to cry, while Georgie Porgie, a real monster, gets away scot-free?

What did Tom do? He stole a pig. As who wouldn't who worked all day in a bakery? Even delicious aromas can revolt one in time. The day comes that one longs for roast pig, and by then only an entire porker can do the job—satisfy Tom's craving for meat and his serious need for protein and electrolyte balance.

The pig was eat, the rhyme goes on to say. By whom? I'm afraid Tom didn't get any. The pig was eat—it could have been by anyone—whereas Tom was beat: we know it was Tom and no other who was beat. And Tom was strong. Have you ever tried to run with a pig in your arms? Have you ever even *seen* a mature pig? I believe the entire town turned out to beat him. It's not fair. Afterward, did he lose his job with the baker? I think so. I think that's why he went crying down the street. No amount of beating could make my Tom cry. He's crying because he lost his job and because the pig was eat before he could get any.

On to Doctor Foster.

"Doctor Foster went to Gloucester / In a shower of rain; / He stepped in a puddle, / Right up to his middle, / And never went there again."

Doctor Foster (a doctor of hydrography, by the way) is a fool. He's a fool to step into a puddle that anyone could see was a yard deep and then because of that one idiotic accident never go to Gloucester again. Did he think that if he went to Gloucester again he would step into a puddle up to his middle and that this was inevitable every time he went there? That would be particularly surprising in a doctor of hydrography. And yet isn't it true? We go to a place, something bad happens, and we never want to go back. Why go back when there are new places to go, where nothing bad has happened, like the Yucatán, which I mention only because that's where I want to go to next.

I wish I could find a rhyme with a man we could all admire. Tom, Tom, even though he's a total sweetheart, is not necessarily admirable (thief and crybaby), and I know you join me in my loathing for Georgie Porgie (craven bully) and my scorn for Doctor Foster (idiot). One would think that nursery rhymes would want to set an example for infants (that's the kind of man I want to be when I grow up; or, that's the kind of man I want to marry), but they don't at all, which is what's so wonderful about them. They know how men really are.

Even in "Jack be nimble; / Jack be quick; / Jack, jump over the candlestick," it is clear that Jack is clumsy and awkward, a stumblebum, in effect.

The candlestick (not many people know this) is not lit. It is not even standing upright in a holder. It is lying on its side on the floor. If Jack could jump over the candle-stick (so pathetic, really), then the idea is that he might go on to jump over a box of soap and thence to the high hurdles at the Olympic Games.

Fat chance. Jack will never make it to the Olympics. No Nehemiah, he. Jack will be a Wepner (the Bayonne Bleeder), and the reason I know this is that I've just looked up stumblebum and it means a second-rate prizefighter.

The more I think about Tom, I think he stole the pig because his lover asked him to, and it was she who ate the pig. Tom wasn't beat up by the townspeople; he was tired. "Tom was beat" means Tom was tired. The whole adventure of stealing the pig and running away with it had wearied him, as who wouldn't it, especially after a long, hard day being a baker's man. No! Now it's coming clear. He didn't work at the bakery at all! He was the *baker's man.* Her lover. He stole the pig and away he ran. To give it to the baker, for whom he'd do anything. Then he was so tired (beat) that he ran crying down the street because he felt bad about not being able to make love to the baker, who, even though surfeited with pig, wanted him to give her a cosmic orgasm.

Wait a minute! I now see that Tom, Tom didn't cry tears down the street. His was a cry of exaltation. He was whooping it up because his whole day had been such a success. He stole the pig, got away cleanly and safely with it, gave it to the baker, they *both* ate it, then they made love. Then, understandably, he was tired (beat), but he still felt great, and damned proud of himself, so he ran crying victoriously down the street, wanting the whole town to see what a man he was. He can be forgiven his vainglory. It is much better than being a fool, a crybaby, or a stumblebum.

A thief he remains. There's no way I can get around the fact, try as I may, that he stole the pig. I deplore crookedness of any kind, which is why (well, partly why) I left Dominic Racatelli.

Too bad. I love Tom. I want to portray him in the best light I can. He's a fast runner (unlike Jack), a great lover (unlike Doctor Foster). He's sensitive and caring and will do anything to please his loved one, even steal for her.

I would want to marry a man like that when I grew up. But if I were the baker, Tom, Tom's lover, I would not ask him to steal for me; I would ask him to kill for me. I would ask him to kill Georgie Porgie.

Watching Adam's appreciative expression, listening to him laugh, Miliana knew that out of all the possible people to select in the English-speaking world, Mother Goose had been right, if not positively inspired, to choose this Argentinian Jew.

"This is something of a paean to Tom Flynn," said Adam, putting the essay aside. They lay at either end of a long couch that was placed before the view window. Miliana saw that the acacia tree was preparing its powdery yellow blooms. Another spring!

"Pee onto Tom? I wouldn't dream of it. Do you think I am a pervert? What a thing to suggest to your mother!"

Adam rolled his eyes, but he was used to his mother's questionable jokes. "A paean is a song of praise," he explicated, although he knew she knew perfectly well what a paean was.

It was twilight, the magical meeting of night and day, of dark and light, a soft drowsy peaceful hour. Miliana could think of nothing nicer than this moment of being with her son. "It's true," she mused, "that writing this essay made me realize how much I do admire, possibly love, Tom Flynn, but he's not a baker's man, he's a firefighter, a fire's man. Tom, Tom, the fire's man," she chanted.

"I've got news for you," said Adam. "The Tom, Tom

16

in the rhyme isn't a baker's man either—he's a piper's son."

"Oh, no!" Miliana was aghast. This was terrible news. She did not doubt that Adam was right, as he had a phenomenal memory. What a shame. Her first piece for Mother Goose, and she was already screwing up. Maybe Mother Goose hadn't been inspired in her choice after all. Maybe she'd made a horrible mistake—in a way that God, in a similar situation, would never have done. For instance, God would not have chosen Abraham to sacrifice his son if he begat only daughters.

But the wonderful thing about Mother Goose, she comforted herself, was that like God she was forgiving and unlike God she was flexible. Miliana took heart.

"Mother Goose won't care," she told Adam. "I'm not going to change it. He'll just have to be the baker's man from now on." She rose from the couch and wandered to the kitchen, where she poured herself a glass of wine to fortify herself in her decision to waffle in her task—to, in effect, do a slipshod job.

Never mind, she comforted herself. Since time immemorial, we prophets have always been allowed some latitude. Every single prophet changed the text a little, and it was allowed, by Whomever, to stand.

While she was at the refrigerator, she got a beer for Adam. Returning to the couch, she looked pensively out the window where the fog, as well as the clouds, was beginning to pick up the colors of the sun, which had set over the Pacific Ocean. Her view looked southwesterly but not west enough for her to witness the actual dropping down of the sun into the sea.

When Adam finished talking on the phone to a friend

17

with whom he was arranging to "pound" some beers, she asked, "Adam, who *was* the baker's man? I'm sure there was one."

"Patacake, patacake, baker's man. Make me some bread as fast as you can."

She laughed, throwing back her head. "I don't think I'll write a paean to anyone named Patacake. Imagine a firefighter named Patacake."

"Is Georgie Porgie supposed to be Dominic?" he asked curiously.

"Oh, no!" she exclaimed, and then had to notice and be interested in the fact of how offended she felt for Dominic and how she then went on to create, not exactly a paean, no, nothing so grand as a hymn of praise, but certainly something resembling a flattering little tune about him. "Dominic wasn't at all like Georgie Porgie. He wasn't a worm, not a detestable type at all. He was an attractive, passionate, intelligent man who played lovely jazz piano."

"But he was a crook?"

"Well, yes, he was."

Miliana chided herself. It was quite unnecessary to have slipped into the essay that bit about Dominic. Why on earth had she done that, she who liked to keep herself private? Now, inadvertently, she had encouraged Adam to be nosy.

"Organized crime?" the boy persisted.

"I guess," she said vaguely.

"Is that why you ran away from him? I never understood about it. You never talk about your past, and I was away at boarding school or with my dad during your marriage to Dominic."

Yes, Miliana remembered, I saw so little of Adam then. Dominic was jealous of my children too.

"I ran away because of his criminal connections and because"—Miliana found herself flushing and was quite amazed at herself, since she was a woman who didn't fluster—"because we loved each other so much. Too much."

"I don't understand."

"It's true I don't like to talk about my past, Adam darling, or even think about it. I live in the moment. But maybe I'll write about it. Maybe it will all come out in my legacy. You'll have to read the next one and see."

She sat down at the upright piano, putting her wineglass on the top. She played "When Sunny Gets Blue" and began improvising on it. *Remember to practice your scales. You must keep strengthening your fingers,* she heard Dominic say, for she always heard his voice when she sat down to play. He had taught her piano playing during those two years they were together, and she had kept up with her playing during the ensuing six years of her ongoing flight from him.

As well as hearing Dominic's voice, she heard Adam's. Adam was talking to her, since he always imagined she could converse and play at the same time. Probably because he didn't really consider jazz music. For him, anything without an amplified guitar and enigmatic lyrics wasn't music.

"Well, keep on writing these things," Adam said encouragingly. "I want to read more. I'll pick you up a *Mother Goose* so you can check out the rhymes as you go along."

"Thank you. That's very thoughtful."

"Is there any reason we can't have the lights on?"

"Yes. I like the dying time of day and don't want to

phony it up. I like to see the sunset unfold, the clouds bloom and color. Is there any reason you can't be quiet while I'm playing the piano?"

"Yes. I don't want to phony it up."

Adam finished his book while Miliana played, and they talked about Fitzgerald during dinner. Adam got ready to go out with his friends, changing one pair of faded jeans for another, and Miliana, too, prepared for departure, changing one pair of white pants for another and pulling on a big V-neck navy blue sweater. "I won't be home until morning," she said, without going into detail.

Miliana supposed that Adam would figure, if he bothered to figure, that she must be going to spend the night with Joel Jarnding, as her nights with Tom Flynn were usually here at her house, where Tom stayed when he wasn't on duty at the firehouse in San Francisco—but if so, Adam would figure wrong. She was off to her night shift on the Suicide Prevention hot line, from eleven to seven in the morning.

This was useful work and work she was good at. It was the only use she had ever been, and she kept it quiet, even from Adam. She didn't want to blow her well-wrought image as a ne'er-do-well. She had worked for Suicide Prevention for years, including the years with Dominic. He had been dead set against her doing it, but that was nothing new; he was against her doing anything separate from him.

On this one score, she hadn't knuckled under. "My mother committed suicide," she told him, "and nobody helped her. Nobody even knew how to help her. I know how to help. I know how to save lives and I'm going to help. I don't see how, by any stretch of the imagination, you can take my putting in this volunteer time to mean I love you less." He did take it to mean that. He couldn't help himself.

He let her go. He succumbed to her insistence on this one thing, but he absolutely forbade her the night shift. A compromise was forged, and she took a day shift. Even then, one of his men drove her to the center and waited for her to emerge four hours later. This was one of the facets of her life with Dominic that became intolerable— her lack of independence, her virtual imprisonment.

Because she liked and needed this "being of use," she had not given up the work even though she realized it was possible that Dominic could find her because of it.

Miliana was so successfully hidden from Dominic, she was almost invisible. She had no charge accounts, so her name could not be found on any ledgers or in any computers. She had no social security card (never having done a day of honest work), no driver's license or checking account. She never signed petitions, no matter how inviting to her sense of outrage. Although a lover of fast, responsive cars, she bought a VW bug convertible that resisted speed and its ensuing tickets. She bought and sold houses and cars in Adam's name, and as her children's surname was Jones, it was pretty impossible for Dominic to trace her through them. Because they had lived with their father during her marriage to Dominic, he didn't even know what they looked like. In time, Adam's running might halo him in limelight and bring him to the notice of Dominic's clipping service, but she certainly wouldn't dampen his athletic ardor on her account. She was not a clipper of wings, least of all Mercury's. Her two daughters had flown away to New York and Paris, with her blessing.

Conceivably Dominic could make calls to suicide hot lines across the country to try to recognize her voice, but it would be a mammoth undertaking and the chances of his happening on the right shift of the right hot line were slim.

Still, she worried. It was the one hole she hadn't covered. And once she was in her chair at the Suicide Prevention center, whenever the phone rang, that feeling of anxiety as to what crisis she would discover on the other end of the line was always combined with the anxiety of hearing Dominic's voice, which would mean that he had found her and her time was up.

three

*M*iliana *was tired the day following* her shift, which was Saturday, and on Sunday she was busy, so it was not until Monday that she wrote the next piece for Mother Goose. Adam, by then, had returned to Berkeley, but in any case she rather thought she wouldn't show it to him, for indeed the legacy was, in subtle ways, stirring up her past, and this essay, "The Old Women in Nursery Rhymes" was far too revealing. It wouldn't just make Adam nosy; it might make him scared.

The old women in Mother Goose's rhymes are not as old as they seem. They are pictured by Arthur Rackham and his illustrating ilk as hideously aged. Their backs are bent, their noses long and warted, and at the end of their arms are particularly horrible hands, which are twice the length of normal hands, with knobbly knuckles and wrists. Raw, red, and worn with toil they are, and if they don't have liver spots on the backs of them it is because while your old society ladies get liver-spotted hands, your regular old working-class, nursery-rhyme women get the red, knobbly, extra-long ones.

The funny thing is that these old women are actually my age, between thirty-three and forty-four. Most of them have young children (although no husbands; we've already seen that there are no men you'd want to marry in nursery rhymes—or anywhere, really). They are vigorous and agile and it is nothing for them to walk twenty miles over hill and dale in all kinds of weather, having endless adventures along the way, all on the pretext of "going to market." If these women were really old, the above would not obtain (the fertility and physical strength).

So here are all these wonderful old women, tougher than nails from going it alone, aged before their time but not *that* aged, thank you very much.

Understandably, women thirty-three years old or forty-four look a lot older than that to a child—or to an illustrator. I am those ages, and it's fair to say that I do have near my nose, sort of under it, not a wart exactly, thank God, but a wen. Also, I have some incipient skin cancers, but then I'm very fair and when I was a young woman, a *younger* woman, we didn't know about the sun's potential for harm and it was a badge of honor to get badly sunburned as soon as we could each spring. My hands, so far, are seven inches long, exactly the length of my face.

The old woman I like best and the old woman I want to be when I get old is this one. Listen: "There was an old woman who lived under a hill, / And if she's not gone she lives there still."

This is a very lovely and mysterious old woman, probably about forty-four years old. It is hard to picture her abode. She does not live at the foot of, in the shade of, on, or in a hill: she lives *under* it.

She's still there (if she's not gone).

Why does she live under the hill and, more important, how?

Again, the illustrators let one down. They try to get around her living under the hill by putting her in a cave, which would be *in* the hill, or by showing the hill sort of overhanging her house in such a way that one could say she lives under it. But hills simply do not do that. Mountains have crags and abutments that would serve to overhang in this way, but hills do not.

No. She is really under it. She has burrowed down and down, way beneath the hill. But her home is not dark and dirty. It is charming. She has electric light with rheostats so it can be any time of day or night. She has radiant heating. She has a stereo and is partial to the music of Charlie Parker and Art Tatum. By way of art she has one large canvas by Mark Rothko and one of David Hockney's shimmering, light-filled L.A. swimming pool pictures.

If you wonder how she has all these contemporary things, it is because she lives there still.

How did she get the money? Well, she once lived with the crooked man: "There was a crooked man, / And he went a crooked mile, / He found a crooked sixpence / Against a crooked stile; / He bought a crooked cat / Which caught a crooked mouse, / And they all lived together / In a little crooked house."

It was after only two years in the crooked house that my old woman began to yearn for the earthen curves of the hill's underness, the peace and the quiet within.

The crooked man did not have scoliosis; he was a criminal. And he went far further than a crooked mile, I'll tell you; he went a good crooked hundred kilometers and on the way "found" mega-sixpences. Yes, his body was straight, but his mind was bent. He liked crooked things all about him. (His old woman wasn't crooked, but she had a way of crooking her finger at him that drove him wild.)

When she left him, she figured that if she fixed up a place for herself under a hill, he'd never find her, and he didn't. He's still looking, not only for her but possibly also for the money of his that she took away with her.

Yes, I'm sorry to say . . . No, I'm glad to say that she, having been given his power of attorney, so greatly did he love and trust her, carefully planned her escape and siphoned off hundreds of thousands of dollars of this money that he had "found." It is accurate to say that since *she* had not "found" any of it, it was not hers to take, but she honestly felt it was only what was owed her after she'd given him a good two years of her outstanding personality. She was not one to go to court with any meanhearted suit. Not for her to play any cat-and-mouse game (crooked cat and mouse) but only to take forthrightly her due and get the hell away.

In the tradition of fugitives, she went underground.

Where she also went is through the money. Have you ever tried to build a house underground? No? Well, let me tell you about it. The bulldozer and the backhoe alone were horrendously expensive. And the labor! She had to get a contractor down from San Francisco, Joel Jarnding, who was the only builder anywhere with balls enough to do the job—to undertake the underhill. What a man! Imagine the problems of ventilation and drainage. He embraced these problems with zest (embraced her with zest as well). Nothing dismayed him. When he hit rock that his jackhammer couldn't penetrate, he dynamited. She came to admire his penetration devices extremely.

The old woman's hill is in San Luis Obispo, a delightful town not far from Hearst's castle. Hearst was another eccentric, who brought a castle over from Ireland piece by piece and rebuilt it *on* a hill. He had a crooked grand-daughter.

Now *Architectural Digest* wants to do an article on the underhill house, but they won't pay her for it, and she needs money. She's supposed to be thrilled to get into the magazine and was told it was tasteless of her to expect an honorarium.

If she did publish, however, it would blow her cover, and she wants to live there still. Meanwhile her cupboard is bare, her records are worn thin, and she's had to relinquish her cleaning lady.

Money aside, living underground has been good for her skin cancers, and the strained look she had from living with the crooked man is gone. She is calm and wise-appearing. Even her hands, now, seem normal-sized, the knucklebones like anyone else's.

Her children are all pretty independent now but love to visit. Joel the builder periodically drives the two hundred miles in his three-quarter-ton Chevy truck to see how the abode is holding up and how the old woman is faring.

Yes, that's the kind of woman I want to be when I get really old (forty-four), if I'm alive and not gone and can live there still.

"Still" does not mean unmoving. No, she's as vigorous as all the old women and goes out each evening at twilight, or in the gloaming, as hill people say, and takes long walks "to market." She's in fantastic shape.

No, "she lives there still" does not mean motionless, by a long shot. What it means is, she lives there quietly, silently, in a hushed environment. There is no noise under the hill except of her own making. The house is still. There is no turbulence or commotion, no weather. Neither is there, as there was with the crooked man, tumult, passion, and pain. There is peace.

I want "she lives there still" to mean she will live there always. But that is the archaic definition of the word. "Still" no longer means constantly, always, steadily, forever. Too bad. In time she will have to move up the coast, north of San Francisco, to abide in a pleasant but definitely exposed house, hidden only sometimes by fog or, once a day, by night.

If she published pictures of the underhill house in *Architectural Digest*, not only would the crooked man find her but the seekers after quietude would bang at her door, wanting in. They are legion, these people who, unable to create peace within themselves, seek it in others, as if it might rub off on them, or were only a tonic to be swigged.

As it is, the editor asked her, "Aren't you the same woman who lived in the little crooked house on the beach in Malibu? You're paler now, and your hands are shorter, but I'm sure you're she who, rumor has it, fled in the dark of night from him who, it is said, never lives there now but won't sell the crooked house and keeps it like a museum while he wanders the globe looking for her."

No, she certainly won't publish. Bad enough that a complete stranger would know so much about her, although naturally she denied she was that woman.

Anyhow, her life is perfect. She has the three children when they visit, the periodic visitations from the dynamite builder, art, music, and the twilight walk.

I wish I hadn't had to sell and move up the coast and could have lived there under the hill always, but then I'd have to place my life a century ago, when the archaic meaning of "still" still stood. And I couldn't have the Hockney, the Rothko, the twilight walk, and probably not the contractor. You can't have everything—sex, art, peace, and immortality too! Still and all . . .

No, you can't have still and all.

When Miliana finished this second part of her legacy, she seemed to hear, over her head, a great flutterment of wings. It could have been a flock of crows, which had lit in the eucalyptus tree that overhung her roof, but she chose to think it was Mother Goose, applauding like crazy.

Therefore she stood up from the drop-leaf table and took a little bow.

I do wish I could show it to Adam, she thought, in the flush of her creative pleasure, but it would alarm him to know that Dominic is hunting down his mother. Also, he might not understand about the money.

Miliana no longer lived in the underhill house, did not live there still because, sensing Dominic Racatelli hot on her heels, she had hightailed it up the coast and across the Golden Gate Bridge to Marin County and the town where Soo Yung Fong, her best friend for many years, had chosen to live. It had not been easy for Miliana to sell so bizarre a house and had taken a large loss, but she had enough money left to buy her present house, one of many doors—the essential requirement for an aboveground fugitive—and to live in financial comfort for a while. The "while" had lasted a year and a half.

A year ago, walking one day on the mountain, she met and began to see a good deal of Tom Flynn the firefighter, but she retained her admiration for Joel the dynamite builder, who, even though he no longer had far to drive, maintained his intermittent visiting style. Now, however, when off the job, he drove a Ferrari, doubtless purchased with part of the money she had paid him for building the underhill house—a *small* part.

To her children, she had alluded only jokingly to her ongoing flight from the crooked man, never admitting to them, and scarcely to herself, that she felt life-endangered, until now, when it was making such a big appearance in her legacy. This is why she decided not to show the piece to Adam.

Her present house was not on a street in a town. It was on a main road that went from one town to another, Mill Valley to Stinson Beach. The road was called Panoramic Highway. It followed the flank of Mount Tamalpais, then traced the foothills down to the sea. Going south, it wound gradually to the mountain's valley before taking the straightaway to San Francisco's Golden Gate Bridge or to the Richmond–San Rafael bridge to Berkeley, where Adam Jones studied and ran.

It was a modest one-story, two-bedroom house, colored white, inside and out. In spring it was adorned with blue iris; in summer, with red geraniums. Miliana was a one-color-plant gardener and nonweeder. Neither did she fertilize, spray, or water. The iris had their brief heartbreakingly beautiful days in the sun and subsided. The geraniums were tough and flamboyant and required no care—her kind of plant (her kind of man too). She took off dead leaves and blossoms to keep them spruce and that was that.

The house had fresh paint and a new roof. It was clean as a whistle and medium tidy. The living room was all glass on one side and looked out at a far vista of trees and hills and sky, often foreshortened by fog, for if ever there was fog from the Pacific, this stretch of road made it its own, the very trees seeming to reach out for it, to draw it over, as if for warmth or cover. It was for its covering qualities that Miliana liked the fog and for the way it altered or disguised the landscape. She felt she was learning from it constantly.

Because the living room walls were subsumed by windows and bookshelves, there were no pictures. In any case, by now she'd relinquished most of her art along with Mrs. Fisk, although she still had a financial ace in the hole in the form of a small Georgia O'Keeffe in the bedroom. She hated to sell beloved paintings, but anything was better than going to work—which in any case she couldn't do without a social security card.

The kitchen was simple and inefficient. The bedrooms were only slightly larger than their beds. There was one bathroom, and on the deck was a redwood hot tub.

This Monday morning, Miliana had gone right from breakfast to writing her essay. Now she saw it was almost noon, and if she didn't get into high gear she would be late for a beauty appointment. She whipped out of her bathrobe, into slacks and shirt, grabbed her purse, and headed out.

four

A*lthough the view out the back* of her house was wild and natural, with no houses in sight, she did have neighbors above her and beside. She shared her parking space with the neighbor to the side: a man with a dog. The dog, a squat brown mutt, liked to snooze in the sun on top of her car. It looked very amusing to see him there, but it was not amusing to try to get him down off the top of the car so she could drive away in it. Starting the engine did not alarm him as it would a cat, say, which would then leap nimbly away. The dog probably was deaf. He certainly did not come when called. In the end, she always had to grab him by the collar and sort of heave him off the convertible top, half strangling him in the process. She did not like to hurt animals or have them act hurt. It was particularly annoying to have to go through this galling ceremony when she was in a hurry, as she was today.

And there he was as usual, on top of her car. "Oh, Lord," she sighed to the dog. "I am not up to it. I am simply not up to wrestling you off the top of my car and getting dog hair all over me and hearing you yelp and yowl as if I were intentionally hurting you."

The mutt raised a weary lid consideringly.

"Get off!" she commanded, pointing at the ground in no uncertain terms. "Now!"

He closed his eyes. The dog definitely had presence. She picked up a stick and prodded him with it. He whimpered but did not budge. His master, whose un-canny hearing made up for his dog's utter lack of it, suddenly appeared beside her. "Are you beating my dog?"

He was one of those fussy old men who are in their twenties. He had no color to his face, hair, eyes, or clothes. Only when he blushed, and she could credit him with having blood in his veins, could she entertain some hope for him as a human. "No," she said, "I am not beating your dog. I am encouraging him to get off my car. I am in a hurry. I do not want to pick him up. He is dirty and smelly and hairy in the extreme."

"You are constantly tormenting my dog." His voice cracked with emotion.

"No, I am not," she said reasonably. "I am an animal lover. I have nothing against your dog. I do not even mind him sleeping on my car roof. I do mind him not getting off when I tell him to."

The man lifted his dog off the car, held him in his arms, and looked at him with dumb adoration. Miliana, observing this, thought sadly, animals are supposed to look at men that way, not the reverse.

"He's old," the man said. "He's been with me for fifteen years."

"I appreciate that you must be very close," Miliana said gently.

"He doesn't get around well anymore."

Only a dog of superior agility could climb onto the convertible top of a Volkswagen bug, thought Miliana, but didn't comment. Instead she said brusquely, again feeling the press of time, "Thank you for helping me out. I suppose there is no way of discouraging your dog from getting up there, but I'd appreciate it very much if you wouldn't let him get onto my boyfriend's car. He's very particular about it" (and is not an animal lover, she thought but did not say).

The boyfriend whose car she referred to was Joel the builder, who had suggested several horrific ideas of how he would like to get rid of this pestilential animal, his favorite one being to drive him across the bridge to the East Bay and leave him there.

"Which boyfriend is that?" the neighbor inquired meanly, as if it were a crime to have two boyfriends, a crime punishable by torture.

"The one with the Ferrari," she said, and with the slightly more massive penis, she would have liked to add but didn't, as it might seem denigrating to Tom. Joel's *was* larger, but who cared? She laughed to herself. Certainly the neighbor didn't. At least she *hoped* he didn't.

She got in the car and drove away. Immediately she forgot about her confrontation with man and dog. Instead she thought, I must write about Mother Goose's animals. Yes! she thought happily. That must be the next addition to my legacy, to my ever burgeoning legacy.

Miliana liked the beauty salon, a small, cheerful place redolent of the aromas of soaps and unguents, operated by essentially homely young women, the homely being drawn to beauty as the unsound are to psychiatry and the unethical to the law. She liked to look at the *Vogue*s and *Glamour*s. As a young woman in Argentina, she had put in a few years modeling, with some success. Her youngest daughter was going that route right now in France. Although much more beautiful, she hadn't Miliana's height, five ten, or confidence. Although had she been confident at nineteen? She couldn't remember.

Miliana had lost touch with her past. It didn't interest her. She was always getting on with life, moving along, leaving no traces. What's done was done; on to the next thing. She looked to the snake, which shed its skin as it grew, sloughed it off as so much waste material.

The salon catered to men as well as to women; this traditional refuge of women, where artifice could be secretly applied, was now invaded. Unlike men, who raised such an idiotic brouhaha when their stupid clubs and restaurants were trespassed upon, the women made no fuss at all, took it in stride, simply pretended the men were women too. A lot of them were.

As usual, she checked out everyone and discounted the chance of anyone's being a threat to her in any way. She knew Dominic would not send another to kill her—he would do it himself—but he *would* send advance parties to find her. The idea, then, was to spot any of the scouting party, likewise any unexpected person who might have known her during those years with Dominic Racatelli as her husband. Such persons were not legion, because he had kept her so much to himself. They'd scarcely ever socialized with other people, except for business (ha ha) friends of Dominic's.

These checks of hers were not any big deal. By now it was second nature to be always on the qui vive.

Just now there were only two people in her life who had known her when she lived with Dominic: her son, Adam, and her best friend, Soo Yung Fong, the only person in the world to whom she could bare her heart.

And Joel. Since Joel had met her soon after her escape from Dominic and become intimate with her during the building of the underhill house, she had confided in him. She regretted now that she had. But she had been in a vulnerable, tremulous state, as one is when released from prison—and as one is even more when having just *escaped*

35

from prison, with the bloodhounds still hot on the scent—
and she had needed someone to lean on.

Tom Flynn knew nothing of Dominic.

Now Miliana, finding everyone there to be harmless,
buried herself happily in the glossies until her turn came.
She loved looking at the newest fashions, although she
tended to dress pretty much the same way year in and
year out: in white pants, cut loose, large soft cotton shirts
from France and Italy, suede running shoes on her feet.
(When it came to the final pursuit, the ultimate chase
scene, she would never be caught in heels.) She had a
suede jacket for the cold and an enormous army trench
coat for the rain. Her wardrobe was geared for comfort
and fluidity of movement, and the large loose clothes on
her tall, full-figured body looked superb, as anyone could
tell her and as she, in any case, knew.

After her haircut, shampoo, lightening, brightening,
and dry, she repaired to a separate room of minuscule
proportions for her lash tint, which was a blue-black dye-
ing of the eyelashes. This required her eyes' being sealed
shut for ten minutes while the dye set.

Alone in the room, she lay on her back, blinded. It
would be hard to dream up a position more open to attack
than this, but as she had already set her mind at ease, she
determined to keep it that way.

However, when, five minutes later, the door opened
and someone entered, all her other senses jumped to the
fore, straining to take the place of her eyes. She waited for
the beautician's voice to say, "Everything all right?" but
there was silence. Whoever had entered was just standing
there.

Standing there emanating hostility thick enough to
take a bite out of.

Miliana felt a distinct menace. This person was not negligible, definitely was one who wished her harm along the order of maiming or killing and she was lying full-length upon a divan, blinded, vulnerable as a newborn baby, an assassin's dream victim.

Although the sweat burst from her pores and her heart accelerated with the rush of adrenaline, she remained outwardly composed. She would not act unless the person moved toward her, and then she would grapple blindly for her assailant. (Even if she forced her eyes open, she would be blinded by the stinging dye.) She could call out, but she was never one to cause a scene, even if her life depended on it. She was a woman of extreme poise. She could, however, and would, address this person, speak softly, perhaps say something intimidating but also ambiguous, something that would lead her or him to believe that despite all signs to the contrary, she knew perfectly well who was there—and so knock the person off center.

She looked toward the door and said, "It's you, is it? What a surprise."

There was a slight movement. She tensed. Then she heard the door open and close. The menace was gone.

Whew! She breathed deeply, willing her pulse to decelerate. She breathed in through her nostrils and out through her lips with little puffs of air, decelerating her mind while she was at it, for it was racing like a hamster on a wheel. Never before had she experienced the emotions of a cornered rat (speaking of rodents), and although generally a person to crave new learning experiences, she had not liked this one one bit, had not learned from it, felt diminished because of it.

Not just a cornered rat, she thought. Worse, a cornered belly-up blinded newborn baby rat.

A few minutes later, the beautician bustled in and began washing her lashes toward the opening of the lids. "Who was it came in a moment ago?" Miliana asked.

"I don't know. I was in the facial room. Now hold still while I put in some drops. There. How does that feel?"

Stepping out the door of the little room, batting her lustrous lashes, Miliana saw the reception desk on her right, and beyond it the larger room for hairdressing. To her left was the door out. The desk was unattended, so she could not ask who had entered her room, or who, perhaps, had entered from outside, for it could have been someone off the street. Actually, she thought not, for how could someone entering know that she was in the little room?

Miliana, still uneasy, paid, tipped, and departed.

For sure, that was her last lash tint. In any case, she was going to have to give up beauty, as part of her financial retreat. This would age her rather rapidly, but it would be temporary, for money always seemed to find its way to her as a dog to its master, knowing its rightful owner.

Usually any such adventure gave her new energy, sharpened her senses and wits, made her feel fully engaged with life. This one, she thought wryly, didn't.

No, she did not feel invigorated. She felt tired. Ailing. Wounded.

Vulnera omnes, ultima necat, was a Latin inscription she had seen on public clocks in England: "All hours wound, the last one kills."

five

To ascertain that she was not being followed, Miliana performed various intricate dodges and maneuvers with the car, before driving on to lunch with her friend Soo Yung Fong, who rented a place in Mill Valley proper, a tiny dim house set deep in the redwood canyon.

Soo Yung, born in Shanghai, had lived most of her life in America. She had been a successful concert violinist, but at the peak of her powers, arthritis had struck her fingers, forever banishing her from the philharmonical kingdom of sound.

At about the same time, her husband, to whom she had been happily married for ten years, died suddenly, leaving her childless, penniless, and deep in grief. She proceeded to make ends meet by giving violin lessons, but her grief, now four years old, was unassuaged. Tragedy had twice cheated her of all her happiness on earth.

Sometimes it seemed to Miliana that Soo Yung's grief had turned to resentment—an ignoble emotion, low on the scale of human feeling. She didn't like to think this, as she loved and admired her friend with all her heart, but the thought would come.

Soo Yung had just finished a lesson, and a tiny child was crossing her palm with a double sawbuck. Miliana thought her friend looked tired and also noticed how thin she was. Was she eating enough? "Let me take you to lunch," she said impulsively. "My treat."

"I have some tuna prepared," Soo Yung said tentatively.

"Save it for supper. My spirits need bucking, and it looks like yours do too."

Soo Yung was the same age as Miliana but looked younger. It seemed to Miliana that Asian women had no middle age. They were young and then they were old—the crossover being at fifty. The same was true of black women, except that they lost their figures in their thirties and Asians didn't. As for blond Argentinian Jews, thought Miliana immodestly, they look stunning until the day they die. But with them it has to do with state of mind. Now, if I were grieving, perish the thought, or if I were feeling that life had done me wrong, I'd look straightaway like an old hag. I know I'd age about twenty years, especially without my hair color and lash tint.

Soo Yung agreed to step out with Miliana. "Just let me quickly change," she said, although, as with Miliana, a change of clothes was an imperceptible change since she always wore an Oriental-style dress with high collar and slit skirt.

She changed from a gray one to a blue-gray one, put her long hair in a sleek bun, and reapplied her makeup. Miliana wore no makeup, having naturally good skin and high coloring.

They went to a sushi restaurant of the town, called Samurai, where they ran the menu's gamut of sushi and sashimi, washing it down with cold Sapporo beer, growing quite lively the while. Behind the bar, the Japanese sushi chefs, with sharp and slender knives, performed their magical ministrations on fresh fish, seaweed, vegetables, and rice. At the same time they set a raucous tone by joking among themselves and their customers, knocking back little cups of hot sake so as to grease their artistry.

In no time at all, Miliana had exorcised the menacing moment in the small room of the salon and was feeling on top of the world. She had the resilience of a rubber band and she absolutely adored eating out. Her first husband, Jones, had been a tightwad and never dined in restaurants. Dominic, although extremely generous, tended to shun public places.

Because Soo Yung looked so worn, Miliana decided not to mention the "cornered rat" incident, even though she usually told her everything.

She did tell about Mother Goose's manifestation in her kitchen, with its resultant burgeoning legacy, two essays of which were under her belt and the third, Mother Goose Animals, percolating away at this very minute. Soo Yung was delighted and encouraging, and desired to read them at once.

"Good," said Miliana. "Adam read the first piece, but I don't want to show him the second, as there is much revealed about Dominic, whom I've come to refer to as the crooked man. I make it quite clear in the essay that Dominic is after me, and I don't want to worry or scare Adam about it."

Soo Yung abruptly changed the subject. "How are Tom and Joel?"

She doesn't want to talk about Dominic, Miliana realized. She thinks I am obsessed with him, but I only mention him so much to her because she's the only one I *can* talk to about him, the only one who knows and can understand the gravity of my situation. Although maybe she never has understood. The thought saddened her, but in fairness to Soo Yung, Miliana reminded herself that in order to fully understand her escape and flight, one would have had to experience personally the terrifying prison of his love, the intensity of this love, and its ensuing metamorphosis into equally intense hatred and relentless pursuit. Okay, Miliana admitted, I am obsessed. But with good reason, Lord knows. Who wouldn't be?

It had been at a reception following a concert of Soo Yung's that Miliana first met Dominic. She had just divorced her children's father and was staying with Soo Yung and her husband in San Francisco. Soo Yung had been asked to solo with the Santa Rosa Symphony Orchestra and Miliana had gone there with her. Dominic, who was weekending in the Napa Valley in order to taste and select wines for the cellar of his Malibu Beach house, had heard of the concert and come.

Miliana remembered how Soo Yung, looking so slight and feminine, had tackled the incredibly demanding Brahms violin concerto with the strength of ten.

At the reception afterward, Miliana's meeting with Dominic was one of those thunderbolt affairs where you lock eyes and, seconds later, lock hearts. He was tall and lean as a knife. He took her breath away. When he smiled, she was disarmed by his crooked teeth. His hair was black and smooth as a raven's wing and his eyes were amazingly like her own, large, heavy-lidded, dark, but his were matte brown and more soulful, hadn't her mischievous glint. Like hers, they were San Paku—eyes that show the white between the iris and the lower lid, a Japanese expression signifying that the possessor of such eyes will die violently, before his time.

"Do you play a musical instrument?" he asked.

"No; I wish that I did."

"I will teach you," he said.

Later, as people were departing, he said, "Don't leave me," and even then Miliana knew that he meant *ever.*

"I won't," she said, and went away with him, not just for the night and not for the "ever" he hoped, but for the two meteoric years. They were married that week.

Now, in Samurai, Miliana sighed and answered Soo Yung's inquiry regarding Tom and Joel, saying, "Tom has gone off to Mexico for ten days with an old friend."

"Girlfriend?"

"Yes. I must say I'm not very happy about it. I was quite surprised at what a loop it knocked me for. I think I'm getting rather fond of Tom."

"But didn't you go off for a weekend with Joel?"

"Yes, I did. I care for them both, you see. And it's for their own good that I do. Loving them both keeps me from loving either one of them too much, which neither of them, established old bachelors that they are, could abide."

"Don't you mean to say it keeps them from loving you too much?"

Miliana smiled gratefully. Soo Yung did understand. "Yes," she said, "that's what I mean. It's probably immoral to have two lovers"—Soo Yung looked as if she entirely agreed with this statement—"but at my age, morals don't matter. What matters is what works. In the end, they'll both go off and marry twenty-year-olds to take care of them in their declining years, which I'm damned if I'll do." Miliana's laugh came from her belly, a full-throated counterpoint to Soo Yung's giggle.

"Maybe you should find a young man to take care of you in your declining years," Soo Yung suggested.

"No, thanks. I'm not planning to decline, and in any case, I've got my kids." No sooner were the words out

43

than she felt bad because Soo Yung didn't have kids for her old age and was already declining, so she turned the words to mean that she didn't like younger men. "I've raised three children; I don't want to raise a fourth, thank you very much. I'll take my men mature."

The arthritis in Soo Yung's hands was deforming them more and more. Miliana wondered if the day would come when she wouldn't be able to use them at all. She wanted to say to her friend, "I'll always look after you, you know. You can count on me for that," but the moment didn't seem right. It would be awkward. She liked to think, to trust, that Soo Yung knew without being told that Miliana would be a loyal friend to the grave, willing to share all she had.

Instead Miliana said, "You are so lucky to have a talent and vocation. The day is coming soon when I will absolutely have to go to work, and I don't know at all what at. Also, as all the world knows, I am so extremely disinclined."

"My vocation is not luck in the least," said Soo Yung, in an aggravated tone. "It is years of hard work and discipline—two things that are anathema to you."

Miliana thought that was rather harsh, although true.

"There's nothing that galls an artist more than to be called lucky," Soo Yung went on, "as if artistry were nothing more than an unexpected inheritance."

"I'll remember that," said Miliana contritely. "You know, Dominic was such a wonderful jazz pianist. I always thought he could have been famous if he'd thrown his heart into it instead of crime. He did have that sensitive side to his nature, which is what attracted me to him initially. What a shame. He could have gone either way. As a piano player he would have been happy."

"Why so? I am not happy. That is another misapprehension people have—that artists, musicians especially, are in some perpetual state of bliss."

"You certainly are feisty today," said Miliana, while thinking to herself, She is determined not to let me talk of Dominic. Why? Well, probably she is bored to death with the subject after all these years. But I need to talk about him. Just to say his name is a pressure release for me. And since I am paying for the lunch, I should be allowed to bore her, at least briefly. Also, I was good enough not to belabor her artistic sensibilities with the "menace in the salon"—although who knows? That might have amused her.

Miliana tended to communicate with people, even her best friend, by way of joking and telling stories. It was hard for her to speak from the heart. In her suicide prevention work, she knew that the only way to understanding was through communication, and she was very good at establishing a rapport with those in trouble, getting them to unburden themselves and find relief. But she was not good at doing this herself. She could be the caring listener at the other end of the line, asking the questions that helped, but she didn't know how to be the one who called. She herself couldn't reach out. It is hard for a helper to ask for help.

"Dominic . . ." she tried again.

"I must be getting back," said Soo Yung, standing up. Her cheeks had the hectic flush that Asians get after a little alcohol. Well, she looks less wan and even a little plumper. Miliana congratulated herself on giving Soo Yung this treat. At the same time she felt sulky about the Dominic deflection.

She felt hurt too. Was Soo Yung, after all these years,

going to begin to disapprove of her? Was she to see her own life as one of discipline, hard work, and suffering, being ennobled thereby, and Miliana's life as one imbroglio after another, inspired only by lust for men, easy money, and adventure—becoming dissolute thereby and generally an object of scorn?

She pursued this difficult inquiry while paying the bill. Maybe, by portraying my life as perpetually endangered, I somehow manage, or hope to manage, to elevate it in my mind, and her mind, into something profound, because it is essentially shallow, trifling, and frivolous.

Mother Goose will know, she thought. I must go to my oracle about all these matters, these pressing matters of love, death, fun, and finance. And animals. I do feel extremely interested to see if Mother Goose has anything to say about dealing with dogs who get on top of one's car and just give you the fish eye when you ask them to get off.

Later, driving up the road to her house on the ridge, she thought about Tom. He had been away in Mexico for five days and she missed him. It would be another five days before he returned.

Suddenly a truck went by and she was forced onto the shoulder of the road, where she stalled. The truck pulled in front of her and Joel leapt out of the cab. Joel never got out of a vehicle; he leapt. He never walked; he ran. He was always on the fly.

"Hi, Max!"

"Hi, handsome."

"Just the woman I wanted to see."

"There are others?"

"How about dinner tonight?"

Having just stuffed herself, Miliana didn't light up at

the idea, but she knew it would be nice to visit with Joel—it had been two weeks since they'd been together, and she was feeling lonely. Nevertheless, she was hot to undertake the next part of her legacy while the creative juices were flowing. "How about tomorrow night?"

Joel scowled and set his jawbone, one of the many fine bones in his excellent face. He hated to plan that far ahead: a whole day. He was a creature of impulse—not unlike herself in that respect. She, however, since she had lived with husbands and children over the years, had learned consideration for others and compromise. Joel had not. "Tonight," he said. "It has to be tonight. I'll come by around six." He grabbed her own fine jawbone and gave her a lingering kiss. Kisses were the one thing Joel sometimes lingered over. Miliana melted. "See you then," he said, and was gone, back into the cab of his truck, whose motor still ran, and away in a cloud of dust before she had opened her eyes.

"Very well," she said to the space where he had been. "Tonight will be fine."

six

That evening, having completed her essay on Mother Goose Animals, Miliana set down her pen and cocked an anxious, even timorous, eye ceilingward.

No congratulatory flutterment of wings this time. Not a whisper. She felt damned abashed. Under the rubric of Mother Goose, she had simply written an essay to ease her heart. Under the guise of enumerating and exploring nursery rhyme animals, she had whined about her boyfriend.

She made a neat pile of the pages, got up from the table, went to the refrigerator, and poured herself a glass of wine. Then she stood by the window, looking out at the melancholy patina of fog. Above it, the evening clouds were taking on the lavender and pink colors of the setting sun, colors that normally could not be considered depressing but managed to achieve this quality now, framed by the gloomy yellow flowers of the acacia.

Miliana glanced over her shoulder, still expecting Mother Goose to appear and take her to task along the lines of shape up or ship out.

And yet she smiled. The truth of the matter was, she felt quite pleased with this piece. Granted she had sniveled about Tom's going to Mexico, but she had said a thing or two too. And made some discoveries, not the least of which was that it looked quite a lot as if she loved Tom and he her—in a good, openhearted way.

She felt enlightened as far as her own life was concerned and more than a little forwarder in her search for the meaning of life via Mother Goose.

It was not in her nature to feel dissatisfied with herself for very long. Three minutes, tops.

She went back to the table and reread the essay with this new attitude. It was called "Nursery Rhyme Animals: Predominantly Pigs (For the Lovelorn)" and went like this:

"There was a woman loved a swine . . ."

Nursery rhymes are full of animals: horses, pussycats, dogs, mice, rats, sheep, every kind of bird, one spider, and a fine array of pigs. Do pigs predominate? If you count the five who, respectively, went to market, stayed home, had roast beef, had none, and cried wee wee wee, probably so.

I choose to say that pigs predominate, as it allows me to write more about Tom, Tom, the baker's man, who stole a pig and away he ran, and who I praised to the skies in a previous essay, and who, at this writing, is in Mexico with another woman.

Now, I don't think of him as the baker's man who stole a pig but as the pig itself.

There is another rhyme, which goes, "Dickery, dickery dare, / The pig flew up in the air." That describes my Tom to a T. Tom thinks he can do anything, even fly. Nothing holds him down. He dares everything. With aplomb. In real life, he is not a baker's man but a fire's man. He is with the San Francisco Fire Department, on the Rescue Squad, which allows him, to his joy, to go into flaming buildings, over cliffs for fallen hikers, into tunnels for subway fires, and underwater for ship fires (or for bodies in cars that drive off piers), and to wade into chemical spills that might explode at any minute into un-quenchable firestorms. What a man!

You see? There I go adulating him again instead of getting down to the bare facts of what a swine he is. But I did want to paint the true picture of his strength and courage, which goes far beyond the mere stealing of a pig for his girlfriend and running away with it, and to show that he is not a thief but a law-and-order man, not a taker but a saver, of homes and lives—a hero, in effect! (I just can't help myself.)

In Mother Goose's day, pigs were much admired. People were more rural then and knew that pigs were the most intelligent of animals as well as affectionate and cleanly. Now, to us urbanites, the word "pig" has come to mean: greedy, dirty, bigoted, and sexist.

Tom is none of the latter and exemplifies the former definition: intelligent, affectionate, and cleanly. He even washes between his toes.

Well, he is *one* of the latter; he is sexist. He likes women as well as men, probably better, but he doesn't think they're as good as men, and the kind of woman he most admires is not one most like a woman but one most like a man—i.e., one who can tie various knots, knows that faucets turn on counterclockwise and that screws and light bulbs go in clockwise, endures pain, doesn't cry, keeps her cool in tough situations, isn't jealous.

When he told me, easy as you please, that he was taking an old girlfriend to Mexico for ten days, I swooned dead away. I was that surprised and hurt (and jealous). It killed me. I actually died for a few seconds, but I didn't have an out-of-body experience with the tunnel, the light, and the joy; I just died.

(Actually, I wasn't that surprised and hurt. I've been

having dizzy spells with or without announcements of impending infidelity from Tom, and I took advantage of a timely one to dramatize the moment.)

When I was breathing again and my blood was going its accustomed rounds, I simply thought, That's Tom for you—the pig who flew up in the air.

He threw Catalina at me. It's true that I had gone to Catalina Island (33°21' north, 118°19' west) the weekend before with my old lover, Joel the builder, but there were, uh, extenuating circumstances, plus Catalina is not Mexico by a long shot, nor is a weekend comparable to ten days by a long shot. What is a long shot? Why do I keep saying long shot? It's because I'm so nervous about this whole Catalina business.

My feeling, understandably, is that it was all right for me to go to Catalina but wrong for him to go to Mexico.

The reason being that he loves his old lover more than I love my old lover. He is still very attached to her and dependent on her.

He says they are not lovers anymore, only friends, but that's what I say about me and Joel.

Why won't he just say, "Bonny lass, pretty lass, / Wilt thou be mine? / Thou shalt not wash dishes / Nor yet serve the swine. / Thou shalt sit on a cushion / And sew a fine seam, / And thou shalt eat strawberries, / Sugar and cream."

That sounds pretty acceptable. I would be his, I wouldn't have to wash dishes, or serve him and his firefighter friends (the swine, get it?).

Oh, if only I hadn't gone to Catalina, then I could feel justifiably wronged. But who wants to feel wronged? Not me. I want to feel loved.

"I'm sorry if I hurt you," he said as he revived me from

my swoon. "What can I say to make it better?" he asked.

"I can think of two things," I answered. "You could say you're not going, or you could say you're taking me instead of her."

He didn't say either. Instead he said, "Goodbye," and went to the door.

"Won't you leave me with something? Some word."

"What if I had asked you for something when you went to Catalina? What would you have given me?"

It occurred to me to say, "My life," but I didn't. I wouldn't really mean it. It would be showboating. And why should you lay down your life for a man who's going off to camp, snorkel, and windsurf with his old sweetheart in Baja California?

Also, to say I would give my life smacks of the same unsavory and unhealthy sort of emotion that obtained during my two years with Dominic, when we truly would have died for each other at any time—when we *wanted* to die for each other to show how great our love was. It may seem to you, if you are a romantic, the ideal kind of love, the perfect love, two hearts that beat as one, either heart guaranteed to stop the instant the other did. But it isn't. I'm here to say, categorically, that it isn't. No, sir.

So Tom left me without another word and I felt hurt and abandoned, even though I honestly conceive of myself as a fiercely independent woman.

How strange life is. Don't you think it's strange?

I look through the nursery rhymes for some answer, some easement of the hurt and bewilderment, some consolation, which great literature is said to give at these times. Others may run to their analysts, throw the I Ching, or decant the port; I to my rhymes.

I trust the answer is to be found among the pig poems,

as that is the theme of this essay, but they seem forlorn of wisdom. Wait, here is one! Yes, I suspect the answer is here: "Sukey, you shall be my wife / And I shall tell you why: / I have got a little pig, / And you have got a sty."

It is terrible but true—how I wish that it weren't—that love is need. Isn't that foul? For Tom to love me, I must, metaphorically speaking, have a sty for his pig, and I am not at all sure that I do. Or that I want to.

I don't want love to be need. I went to Catalina with Joel to show Tom I don't need him, to show him that I love him for himself, for his courage and humor and gentleness, not for what he can give me emotionally, physically, or financially.

Conversely, mightn't he have gone to Mexico for the same reason, to show that he loves me for my gentleness and humor?

Not by a long shot, you are thinking. But you are wrong. That is exactly why he went. It's as clear as day. He loves me madly and doesn't love her at all. He only needs her sty to put his pig in. Hmmm.

Never mind. Here's what I'm going to do.

"There was a lady loved a swine. / Honey, quoth she, / Pig hog, wilt thou be mine? / Hoogh, quoth he."

If Tom, upon his return, ecstatic at seeing me again, should say, "Wilt thou be mine?" I shalt throw my arms around him with all my accustomed ardor and say, "Hoogh!"

What does "Hoogh" mean? you may ask. It means, Hell, no, I will not be yours. But I will love you for the fine brave honest man that you are and you can always count on me and I will be as good to you as I know how to be.

As long as I can get the pronunciation down, that is.

I rather think, since it is a pig quothing, that one should expel air through both nostrils whilst making the *hoogh* noise deep in the throat. This isn't easy. Nothing that's hard is. Mother Goose is demanding, but through her I am consoled and enlightened. Through her I learn love and forgiveness and generosity of heart. Hoogh!

"Hey, Max, how long have I been sleeping?"

She turned to see not Mother Goose emerging from the bedroom but Joel. He was naked, brown from the waist up, with pale loins and moderately hairy legs.

After Dominic, no man looked hairy to her. Dominic's skin cover wasn't hair, it was fur, and it abounded. She'd been shocked at first. He took her breath away for the second time that night of their first meeting. And there was a third time too, because all that hair meant a lot of testosterone. The man had been outside her experience.

"You slept a couple of hours," she answered Joel. "You were tired. I'm glad you had a little nap."

He ran a hand over his thick brown hair, which, she saw with a pang, was going gray. He was a medium-sized, muscular man in his early forties, who stood with his legs wide as if balancing on a high beam, and with his broad shoulders slightly forward, preparatory to leaping through the high air onto another beam.

"Let's go out to dinner somewhere nice," he suggested.

"Why don't you let me cook you a little something here?"

"Why should you? You're always here. I want to take you out. You look like you could use some fun."

He's giving me a treat because I look so poorly, she

thought. Just as I did for Soo Yung. I wonder if everyone takes friends out to dine just because of pity.

"Get dressed. Let's go."

Miliana could tell he was upset that he'd slept, that he'd shown himself so human as to be tired, this superman. Also, he probably felt he'd let her down by conking out and now wanted to make amends by giving her a night on the town, when she was really more than content to linger here in her bemused state, one with the fog and the dreary sunset. She felt like being alone with Joel and quiet.

He pushed her toward the bedroom. "Get dolled up. Wear the green shirt I gave you last Christmas."

"That was about five Christmases ago, but never mind."

"Have I known you that long? I wonder what I see in you."

"I'm the only woman who can put you to sleep," she said complacently.

"I'll say!"

When, fifteen minutes later, she joined him outside, she found him with the neighbor's dog in his hands, raised high over his head as if he were about to dash it to the ground and stomp on it. The dog, not in the least anxious about his unusual situation, looked, if anything, bored.

But Miliana panicked. "No!" she cried, running to the scene. "Give the dog to me." She held out her arms imploringly.

"What? And get you all dirty? What's the matter with you?" But he dropped the dog down on all fours instead of flinging him away to the next county. He then glared at the animal, who, maintaining his self-possession, walked away on stiff, stumpy legs. Joel aimed a kick at him and missed, owing to Miliana's knocking him off balance. He turned his glare on her. "I've had it with that dog climbing all over my car." He ran a hand over the top of the Ferrari as if to see whether it was bleeding.

He was in a foul humor, Miliana realized. But he almost always was these days . . . these years. He worked too hard. He was driven. By now he should have a team of men to build houses for him, but nobody was good enough. He had to do it himself, with just a helper or two. He was a perfectionist. He built quality houses that he sold for half a million and were worth more. He worked seven days a week, from dawn to dusk, regardless that he'd made his million twice over. Also, he liked to say that he didn't want to have a lot of men financially dependent on him or he wouldn't be able to take off a month when he wanted to. But did he ever take a month off? He had taken a weekend to Catalina. That was the only vacation she knew about in the last year.

"I spoke to my neighbor about it this morning," Miliana said soothingly. "I particularly asked him to keep the dog off your car. It's hard to know in these cases whether to blame the dog or the master. I do think this dog gets a real kick out of annoying us, but I can't help but be impressed at how well he succeeds. One is always on the defensive with the damn mutt."

They got into Joel's car, where, taking the hairpin turns at seventy, he seemed to begin to relax.

Miliana pursued the subject. "I feel like I could learn a lot from that dog. He's completely unflappable."

Joel snorted. "You learn from everything. The last time I saw you, you were learning from the fog."

"It's true. I do learn from the fog. You'd be surprised."

At dinner in a restaurant in Tiburon, where a view of San Francisco and the bay made Miliana feel overexposed but where Joel became genial, she was burned by a pair of wounded eyes from across the room. They were centered in the face of a woman dining with a blond young man.

"An old girlfriend of yours?" she inquired, gesturing toward the table.

Joel looked and flushed slightly. "How'd you know?"

Miliana felt cheered. It occurred to her that the menace in the beauty salon had not been one of Dominic's vigilantes but simply an old or, more likely, a current girlfriend of Joel's (or even Tom's), who had learned about Miliana and was murderously jealous. It could have been a customer or even one of the dun-colored little beauticians. Miliana, prideful old pro that she was in dealing with danger, was humiliated to think that some jealous fool had so terrified her. Never mind that she was blinded at the time, like Samson Agonistes.

Well, she'd carried it off all right, banished the menace from her presence. Still, it was stupid not to have considered the jealousy angle. What if she *was* obsessed about Dominic and had allowed his pursuit of her to the death loom so large in her mind that she was imagining him behind every bush and light pole, in every view of the city.

But how annoying to be set upon by these "other women." It was Tom who was chronically faithless, who had terminal Lotharioitis. For sure, the beauty shop experience involved some little idiot friend of his.

"I can't make her out very well, but she's probably foreign." Miliana peered across the room at the offending eyes. "You've never liked native-born Americans. Does she perchance work at Bella's Beauty Salon, this girlfriend?"

Unlike Tom, who was honest to a fault, Joel was a master of evasion. "You're my girlfriend, Max," he said.

Now might be a good time to disabuse him of that notion, she thought, full of wonder that he could imagine a woman as loving and affectionate as herself would be content with a twice-a-month boyfriend.

While Tom knew about Joel, it had always seemed the better part of valor not to trouble Joel with any particular knowledge of Tom. He was not as easygoing.

"Aren't you my girlfriend?"

There was something ominous about his tone of voice, his look. . . .

Oh-oh! What had she done with that essay when she went to the bedroom to get dressed? Might Joel have read it? If so, would it sound like gibberish or would it sound as if she was in love with a fireman named Tom even though she also saw, and went to Catalina with, a builder man named Joel?

She looked keenly at Joel, but he had already learned from the dog, or from someone, how to shutter his eyes and give nothing away. If he had read the essay, it would explain his excessive anger at the dog as anger meant for her.

Miliana felt beset, but when he repeated his question, "Aren't you my girlfriend?" she remained fairly unflappable.

"In a manner of speaking," she answered.

On the way home, Miliana realized they were being followed. It was a large Chevrolet unusual to see in this county of foreign cars. Tom had a Chevy, but of course he was in Mexico. She could mention the tagalong vehicle to Joel, who then with his mighty sports car could easily lose it, but more likely, in the mood he was in, he'd say she was imagining things and slow down to torment her. When they got to Miller Avenue in Mill Valley, she asked Joel to stop at the 7 Eleven so she could pick up an item. Getting out of the car, she looked to see what the Chevy would do, but the lights she'd thought were it weren't. Either she'd imagined it or the man was good.

When she got home and said good night to Joel, she waited outside until he drove off. She watched the road. Shortly, a big American car appeared, which could have been the Chevrolet. It was heading back down, which meant it might have seen Joel turn in at her house, passed on by, then turned. Damn. Someone who had not known where she lived, and wished to learn, now had.

The neighbor's dog was a plump black shadow on the top of her car. Miliana sighed deeply, then, taking a last look at the stars, went into her house.

She did not see Joel return.

Inside, she stood thoughtfully by the table where the pages were piled, face down, and studied their configuration. At the end of her reading, she would have gathered them up, stood them on edge on the table so as to align them, then put them down just as they were now. If she'd been standing by the chair, that is. But she'd been sitting in it. Whereas Joel would have picked them up from where they lay on the table in front of the chair and read them standing. He never sat down, except to eat or drive.

In short, it seemed to the canny eyes of Miliana that these scribbles regarding nursery rhyme pigs had been put down on the table (back down) by someone standing and approximating the place where they had lain before he impulsively reached for them.

Miliana sighed and went to the piano. Her nepenthe. When Dominic had taught her the chord changes and the way to improvise melody, he'd said, and was saying to her now as she sat down, *The melody is your line drawing, the chords are your color and texture. Keep the beat in your head and go for it.*

Although she always heard his voice, she never conjured up his face and form. Six years would not have changed him very much, she thought now. He'd only be forty-five. Time's winged chariot still did not have him by the short hairs. Joel, almost the same age, had gone gray as if overnight. She smiled. Dominic would not go gray. Or fat. Or ugly. He was a lot like an Argentinian Jew in that respect, was Dominic—a stunner to the grave.

Miliana placed her hands on the keys, thumped her foot on the floor, counting one two three four, and went for it.

seven

If one has been pursued by an enemy of the caliber of Dominic Racatelli and successfully eluded him for six years, then one doesn't worry much about jealous females, and Miliana wasn't too concerned about Joel's jealousy either. She felt sorry for anyone caught in the coils of the green-eyed monster. It was no fun to be there. It was never any fun to be in an unnatural state of mind instead of having all your wits about you. Who wants to become weak, and idiotic, and driven? She herself, she realized, had succumbed for a moment to the monster's fetid breath when Tom had told her of his Mexican vacation, but that wasn't just jealousy, she told herself, it was hurt and the feeling of being abandoned, less favored, less loved. Right? Wrong. It was jealousy.

Jealous people, thought Miliana the next day, while taking her customary late afternoon walk on the mountain, do a lot of stupid, harmful things, but they rarely kill you. They think the world would be a much better place without you and they want to kill you, but they don't because they're not so crazy that they'd risk going to jail and being murdered themselves, either by justice, in the guise of capital punishment, or by other prisoners, who, if they don't kill or maim you, will, minimum, sodomize you.

So thought Miliana. But as the days went by, she began to wonder if she shouldn't revise her ideas about jealous people. Perhaps they weren't so determined to avoid death and sodomy after all, for it did definitely seem that she was being stalked by one of them.

The incidents were odd but somehow chilling. One time, she was downtown doing her marketing, and when she returned to her car with the bundles, the top was down.

It gives a person pause to park her car with the top up and return to it fifteen minutes later, to find that the top is down. It's spooky. It doesn't hurt you or the car, but it is a signal. Someone is tampering with you and they want you to know it.

Miliana was twenty yards away when she saw the VW's transformation, and she didn't break stride. She stowed her bags in the trunk and got in the car as if nothing were amiss—since very likely the top-tamperer was lurking about to catch her reaction, and she was determined to disappoint him (or her).

Another time, she came home and on her doorstep was a crushed animal, an animal that had been run over by a car. It was not all blood and guts; it was a dried-up carcass of some vermin, which now looked like a rough-hewn Frisbee. This time she did react. Her impulse was to reach down, pick it up, and fling it away, and she acted on the impulse, but if he was watching, her harasser would have been disappointed this time too, for she made it look like fun. The carcass, like a Frisbee, took flight. In a soaring arc, in a glittering whirl, it spun away into the blue.

However, it was not fun. It was not nice to find a piece of roadkill on her stoop, and the signal here was: Not only do I know your car; I know your house.

It wasn't funny either. Although the converted car top

could be taken as a joke—by Joel, say—the dead animal was not funny. Not by a long shot.

The third incident could not be construed as a joke or even an unpleasantness. It was an attempt on her life.

Miliana always kept the temperature of her hot tub rock steady at 108 degrees and accordingly plunged in with a blithe spirit. A woman of regular habits, she always took her hot tub in the evening, after her walk on the mountain. This evening, a Friday, she disrobed and, by the merest fluke, a letter fell out of her pocket and into the tub, and it was while reaching for it that she burned her fingers. Astounded, she withdrew the thermometer. It was 119 degrees. Someone had tampered with the thermostat.

Miliana pressed her lips together. She was more angry than frightened. More than either, she was disappointed not to have her tub to ease her old bones after her hike, which had seemed quite tiring and long—maybe because the fog had come in and there was nothing to look at but mist, or maybe because it had been such a horrible, horrible day.

Today she had broken up with Joel.

Yes, after all these six years of loving Joel the builder, she had ended it forever. It wasn't because of Tom, who was still in Mexico, having the time of his life. Unbelievably, it was because of the neighbor dog. Since her Monday-night date with Joel, the week had passed without her once having to contend with the mutt sleeping on the top of her car. She hadn't seen hide or hair of the maddening creature. She began to miss him and then to feel concerned about him. At first she thought the neighbor man was away and the dog with him, but he wasn't. She often saw him skulking around in his colorless way. Could the dog be ill? She hoped to encounter her neighbor and ask, but he seemed to be avoiding her. In one glimpse she had of him, he seemed terribly altered, like a man disturbed, a man grieving. Then she had the terrible thought that Joel had fulfilled his threat of driving the animal across the bridge and leaving him on the other side, to wander through the East Bay like a shade, no way to cross back to Marin. She remembered how furious Joel had been with the dog on the occasion of his visit to her.

She had to know if this was so. Since she had established herself as a partisan of the dog during Joel's encounter with it, she couldn't worm the truth out of him by pretending she was pleased that her problem with the beast was over. If she outright accused Joel of doing so really vile a deed, he would deny it. She would just have to search him out, express her true concern, and hope that he would level with her.

Currently he was building a house in Mill Valley, on the ridge above Blithedale canyon. She drove over to the site and found him and one of his men unloading lumber from the truck. The job had reached the framing stage. She stood by the truck, enjoying the fragrance of the wood and the efficiency of the men's moves. One of the great pleasures of her recent years was watching Joel build houses. From the clearing of the site to the pouring of the mud (concrete) to the last lick of paint in the interior, it fascinated her. Now she had a forlorn sense that she would not see this one to its completion.

Joel took a break and they drifted away from his worker. "Joel," she said, achieving just the right reasonable tone and equable air she had practiced for the confrontation, as if she were interested but not seething inside, "I'm concerned about the disappearance of my neighbor's dog. I know you were annoyed with it the other night, understandably, and I'm afraid, as some sort of retributive measure, you've taken it away across the bridge."

"That's right; I have."

Even expecting this, Miliana was shocked. She felt her pulse beat go up and heard the roar of water in her ears. True, there was a stream going by below where they stood, but it was babbling, not roaring like the one in her ears, which wasn't going by but was going down, as water roaringly does in a fall or when cascading over boulders.

Having ascertained that the roar was definitely in her ears, she tried to ignore it. "Did you leave him across the bay?" She strove to stay reasonable until she got the facts, although she suspected she was shouting over the inner-ear waterfall or cascade.

She hoped that she wasn't going to have a dizzy spell. This was not a moment she wanted to dramatize in that way.

"Yeah. I did."

Miliana envisioned the poor old mongrel, separated from his master probably for the first time, in unfamiliar territory, his failing senses unable to direct him home even if home were accessible, the way not barred by an incomprehensible bridge. It wrung her heart. And the poor neighbor man! To lose his pet in that way, not to know what had happened to his companion of so many years, his best friend.

Her voice trembled, but her words were stern. "I will go to the Humane Society there and see if the dog has shown up. They don't kill them for a week. Maybe I'll be able to find him and bring him back. As you are my friend, I feel the responsibility is mine—but, Joel, I can't forgive you for this. You have done a cruel thing. Very cruel. Unforgivably cruel."

He shrugged and looked over at the lumber, wanting to get on with it.

Perhaps it was the callous shrug that made her say, much to her own surprise, "I don't want to see you anymore."

"Are you kidding? Because of a dog? A smelly old mutt like that, who made your life a misery every time you wanted to go somewhere?"

"One has to be decent."

"You're a fine one to talk about decency. You and your fireman. A fireman!" he exclaimed, as if that were the lowest of the low.

So he *had* read the pig essay.

She was not going to be thrown on the defensive. She again strove for the reasonable tone and achieved it, although there was no question now but that it was a shouting tone too. "I believe we've had an understanding over the years that we were free to see other people. I'm not your wife."

"I'll say you're not!" he shouted back. She wondered if *he* had a waterfall in his ears. "Didn't you ever ask yourself why I never married you?"

"No," said Miliana truthfully, for she never once had. He went on as if she'd said yes.

"Do you think I could ever trust you as my wife?" His face began to be flushed with what seemed to be a mounting anger. "Do you think I would marry a woman who robbed her husband?"

"Robbed!" Now Miliana felt *her* face flush hotly. Robbed! What did he mean? She'd only taken her due from Dominic.

"Yes, robbed." He thrust his body forward and waved his arms. "You're a thief. Nothing more than a common thief."

"I simply took what fairly belonged to me. I could have gone to court and had it awarded to me, but I didn't choose to drag Dominic through the mud, or draw the government's attention to his vast untaxed wealth. I had that much respect for him and his privacy."

"You think you're so great, so special, set apart from others with your own rules. You can do anything, and it's all right. But I can't."

All this was getting pretty venomous. The man was hurt, she realized. She'd hurt him by saying it was over and by telling of her love for Tom in the pig essay.

"And even so, you're just using the dumb dog as an excuse. It's because of the fireman you're breaking it off with me. I'm not such a fool I can't see what's in front of my face."

He's not hurt so much as his pride is. Yes, it's his pride that's hurt. The fact that I love another more than I love him, and that the other is a fireman, which he considers to be a lowly profession, even though it is in fact a noble one, the noblest of all. Well, one of the noblest.

Of course, I never felt humiliated when he had a girlfriend in a lowly profession, since I myself have no profession. Miliana thought of the girlfriends of Joel's she knew about, doubling it by the number she didn't, and wondered at the hypocrisy of the man, but again she credited him with his hurt, remembering her own torment at Tom's going to Mexico with another, even though she regularly saw Joel.

"A fireman," he said again, but this time it was more a disgusted mutter than an exclamation.

"I also have a lover who's a garbage man," she said.

"I believe it," he said grimly.

"I gave up the street sweeper, cute though he was. One has to draw the line somewhere." She put a hand on his shoulder. "I'm sorry if I've hurt you. I never intended to. I've always been your loving friend. If I've cared for others too, it never diminished my love for you or did you harm in any way. I hope and believe I've always been there when you needed me. But you've changed. You're not as nice as you were and I am undone about the dog."

"You can't stand it that I see through you, that I know the woman you really are. You have it coming to you, Miliana, and you'll get it too. I don't know how you've escaped so far. Yes, I do. You take everyone in with your beauty and your charm. But you're not as young as you were. You're going gray, I see."

"No, I've just stopped tinting my hair, so I'm not going, I've already gone, just as you have." Only you've also gone mean, she added silently. "I've stopped coloring it because I can't afford the beauty parlor. I'm broke as can be, quite desperate. I shall have to find someone to rob, common thief that I am, who's lost her looks."

And with that, she turned and departed.

Miliana went immediately to the East Bay pound in Oakland and looked through chain-link cages at dogs of every description, but no brown, fat, short-legged, deaf dog was there to greet her with his baleful look. The more she thought about him, the more her heart was wrung. She left her name, phone number, and a handsome bribe with a dogcatcher named Fred—a sturdy, stone-faced, leathery little man, not unlike the dog himself—and urged him not only to let her know at once if the dog was caught but also to look for him especially. "I'll catch the little blighter," he vowed, somehow giving Miliana the impression of a knight of old, going to slay the dragon for his chosen princess. "He don't have half a chance. I'm the best dogcatcher in Alameda County."

"I'm delighted to hear it." She decided to fire his ardor. "You are up against an unusual canine, however. He has uncanny powers. Good luck!"

Then Miliana had gone home to her tiring mountain walk and the attempt on her life.

Forgoing the tub, then, she took a shower, poured a glass of wine, sat down before her fogbound view, and began to cheer up. Through the veil of fog she saw the merest suggestion of shapes, which her memory served to make into statements: of plum tree, near hill, far hill, eucalyptus, acacia. She tried to see it without her memory and couldn't. She sipped wine and her mind roamed. She had a happy thought that all her recent symptoms of fatigue and dizziness, her feeling diminished, ailing, or wounded, could be menopause, rather than something chronic or fatal. It was certainly time. Then her spirits were lifted further when her beloved son, Adam, walked in the door, home for the weekend!

He was buoyant with plans, and when she heard them she began to get depressed again.

eight

After an exchange of greetings and a brief rundown of their respective news of the week, Adam told her how he and some of the other men on the Cal track team had decided to run a "preppy mile" and establish a world record for the *Guinness Book*.

Miliana got up and refreshed her wine. She returned to the couch, her son, and the fog, which was so dense now that it did not even suggest shapes for her memory to enhance. Nor was there any hint of sunset colors struggling to illuminate the gray; it was simply getting dark. The windows were wet and she could hear the trees dripping. The sodden yellow acacia blooms, beaming blurrily, were the only color. Or was that supplied by memory? And desire?

"Instead of wearing shorts, singlets, and spikes," Adam continued enthusiastically, "we'll wear button-down shirts, ties, khaki pants, and penny loafers. We're thinking maybe we should carry briefcases too. What do you think?"

"I think that would take away the preppy purity. It would become the fastest encumbered mile in that case (in that briefcase), or it would assume the proportions of the fastest brief mile or—"

"Mom, this isn't a joke!"

"It isn't? Pardon me. What on earth is it, then?"

Adam scowled. "Well, it's a fun idea, but we're talking about some of the best runners in the country here, too."

"I see, which is why I am to show respect for this idiocy."

"I show respect for your Mother Goose essays, which are essentially idotic."

"That's true." Miliana felt justly reprimanded and, as he had felt at her remark, hurt and insulted.

Miliana had reckoned that the day would come when Adam's running talent would put him on the sports page in boldface and thence to Dominic Racatelli's clipping service. She was prepared to be generous-hearted when the day came, but it did seem a shame that he had to bring attention to himself prematurely in this capricious way, delightful as the idea, she had to admit, was.

She couldn't blame him. He didn't know the truth of his mother's precarious existence and how he would jeopardize it all for a lark. Should she confide in him? He was a grown man now. Why not have him help shoulder the burden? she thought dubiously. Maybe he could help her, advise her. After reading her first Mother Goose piece, Adam had asked her about Dominic. Perhaps she should let him see the second piece, "The Old Women," wherein she told about her flight from Dominic and her hidey-hole under the hill.

Or, since the preppy mile was still in just the talking stages, maybe she should not concern herself yet. Often that was the sort of idea that was more fun to talk about and plan than actually do.

Then she hit on a bold stroke. "It is a wonderful idea, Adam, but what about your earring?"

His hand flashed to his left ear, where a small gold ring was impaled. He had astonished her and his sisters by this permanent adornment, he being so conventional and so earnest about his appearance. But ever since he was a little boy, he'd enjoyed doing the unexpected and throwing his family off center.

"I do believe that earring would make you inadmissible for this mile. It is subversive to the preppy stance. Even if you took it out, the hole would remain as a giveaway to the keen of eye, and I believe the *Guinness Book* looks very thoroughly into these things."

"Hmmm. I'll have to decide which is more important, the earring or the mile. If the mile, then I can begin right away to grow the hole back together."

Miliana smiled. She had bought time. It was something she had learned in her years of suicide prevention work, to buy time until the person got over the crisis, to make a contract, if possible. In this instance, it would not be appropriate to make a contract with Adam not to run. Not running a preppy mile was not the same as not committing suicide, even though this mile could lead ineluctably to her own death.

Of course, everything led to one's own death; it was just that some things led more quickly.

This train of thought reminded her that she had her suicide shift that night and had promised herself, before she went off, another hard look at her finances, with a side glance to Mother Goose to see what she might recommend. Miliana must figure out how she was going to live for the next little while, in the style to which she was accustomed now that she was accustomed to scrubbing the floor again. She owned her house and car outright, so there were no payments, but there were taxes and food and fuel for the car and tuition for the kids and . . . and . . . and . . .

"Sweetheart, would you be a lamb and make dinner for us? I have another of my idiotic essays to write before I go off for the night."

"Sure. What have we got?"

"Salad makings, fresh corn, fresh sourdough bread, pastas galore—be inventive."

"Name me some meat."

"Sorry; I forgot you were coming. But there's a package of Italian sausage you can consider."

Adam, with the sausage and the salad makings, created a pizza, making the dough himself, while Miliana started her new essay. She broke for dinner, went to the hot line, and finished the essay in the morning, upon her return.

It was called "Finding a Career Through Mother Goose" and got rather out of hand.

" 'Jacky, come give me your fiddle, / If ever you mean to thrive.' / 'Nay, I'll not give my fiddle / To any man alive. / If I should give my fiddle / They'll think that I'm gone mad, / For many a joyful day / My fiddle and I have had.' "

Jacky is my kind of boy. I have never worked. I have fiddled my life away. By this I don't mean I am a musician. No, I'm a trifler. I'm not a stumblebum like Jack Be Nimble, but I am, like the Jacky above, a good-for-nothing time-waster and non-thriver.

My history, briefly, is this. I married young and my husband supported me and our three children, as was customary in those days. Then, when he grew critical of my fiddling and began constantly to moan about being on a treadmill and having to support us all, I divorced him and subsequently married the crooked man. We lived together for two years in our crooked house with the crooked cat and mouse on Malibu Beach in fat city.

Then, as I came to understand his deeply felonious nature, I made my getaway from him, repairing to a house under a hill, where I wish I lived still but whence, being a fugitive, and the money getting low, I had to move on.

I bought myself a modest cottage in Marin County, where I hoped to continue fiddling my days away on the money from the sale of the underhill house. However, that money, too, was soon gone. What to do? I wondered.

Marry again? I think not. I hate to be criticized, and it does seem to be a prerogative of husbands who are supporting you to do that. You'll say I shouldn't generalize from that one bad experience with my first husband, but from where else is one to infer home truths if not from experience, especially bad ones. Don't generalize at all, you say? As well say: Don't think, have no opinions, form no conclusions. What a barren life of the mind that would be. It is you, too, who would have me make no sweeping statements or wild surmises, you who would take away Jacky's fiddle and bid him thrive.

"My little old lady and I fell out. / I'll tell you what 'twas all about: / I had money and she had none / And that's the way the noise begun."

How I deplore fighting, and fights about money are the worst. What cruel fights they are. How small, mean, and nasty those who engage in them become. Again, that only obtained in my first marriage. Dominic was a prince about money and not simply because he had so much of it. Amount is rarely at the root of such an attitude. But Dominic and I fought bitterly about other things. Our value systems were hopelessly different and, as well, I raged against his love, which tried to consume me.

Tom and I never fight (that will be my dear friend Tom, Tom, the fire's man), never exchange one bitter word. We are nice to each other, kind and considerate. Tom understands fiddling perfectly. That's why he needed a job that could catapult him into action with a great tintinnabulation of bells and howling of sirens. It's perfect. He's on duty twenty-four hours and off forty-eight or seventy-two or ninety-six before going on again, and even while at the fire's house, he can fiddle between fires.

When we are together, we talk and laugh and tell stories, often while walking miles of mountain trails. Sometimes he goes diving for abalone, and from the shore I watch admiringly what little I can see of him, behind the veil of glittering sea foam that ricochets from the rocks where the abalone cling and where Tom is being tossed by the sun-spangled waves. We cook scrumptious meals, and when they are eaten, we both clean up. I play the piano, he listens. We play chess badly. We sit silently together, watching the fog. We don't accomplish one single thing. It's an art.

This is how I lived with Tom until the time came when I simply had to go to work. The kids were still in college and not ready to support me, as I have trained them to expect to have to do.

What was I fit for? What could I do? Here I was, forty-four years old, with no background in anything.

Naturally I went to my Mother Goose, to see what I could find. There are dairy maids and lads who are minders of pigs and sheep and cows, such as Little Boy Blue (come blow your horn) and Little Bo-Peep (has lost her sheep), but Marin County isn't that rural, except way to the north, and also it seems like you don't much see boys and girls in the corn or pasture or meadow, minding swine and kine anymore, like you used to—and certainly not any forty-four-year-old women, specifically Argentinian Jews with beautifully manicured hands.

But Mother Goose didn't let me down. She never does. Here's what I found. The very thing! "If I'd as much money as I could spend / I never would cry old chairs to mend, / Old chairs to mend; / I never would cry old chairs to mend."

"That's it!" I exclaimed. "I'll mend chairs." I read the rhyme to Adam.

"Please, Mom," said my son, Adam, the conservative child of the three, a lovely, slender, blond boy, good as gold, all enveloped in Ralph Lauren. "Don't go through town crying, Old chairs to mend, old chairs to mend."

"But why not? It's something I can do, that I'm good at. I can wicker, I can cane. I can upholster and reupholster, replace springs and stuffing. Everyone has old chairs in their attic. I myself do. There is no overhead to speak of: a little glue, a few tacks. I could even grow the cane and wicker in my garden. What is wicker?"

"Twigs from willow trees," he said—a little sullenly, I thought.

"How wonderful! We already have a willow tree. What luck! All we need, then, is a canebrake and some glue."

"I just don't want you to go through town calling, Old chairs to mend."

"It seems like that would be the fun of the thing, honey, a way of getting out and about. Plus, what better or cheaper way to advertise?"

Suddenly he got a light in his eyes. Good, I thought, he's coming around. But no; he said, "What about the crooked man?"

"What about him?" I asked guardedly. It would seem that Adam had availed himself of my second Mother Goose essay on his own, or how would he know my new nickname for Dominic? This very evening, apparently, even as I write this work essay, he has found my sequestered works and learned them by heart. It would seem there was an ongoing raid by all my friends and family on my Mother Goose writings, everyone perhaps hoping to find the key to me. (Soo Yung had come by the house one day when I was out and read them all—the first three. Granted, I'd said she could. Still! Still and all . . .)

"Your visibility," Adam answered. "You want to be lying low so he can't find you."

"The last place in the world he'd look for me would be mending chairs. I could shout Old chairs to mend right in his face and he wouldn't know me. I'm not sure *I'd* know me."

"Well, I wouldn't want to know you," Adam said, pretty much laying it on the line.

I ignored this. A boy can't be expected to understand how few the options are for an older woman going to work for the first time in her life, in a world no longer rural.

The next morning, home from my hot line shift and still wide awake, I ate a bowl of cereal and blueberries, drank heaps of coffee, then called to the still-sleeping Adam, "I'm off to the nursery now for cane seedlings. I've always wanted to raise cane. Ha ha! Come to think of it, let's not forget rush-bottom chairs. I could plant rushes in the marsh back of the school. Do you suppose the nursery would have rush seedlings?"

"Never in a million years," he replied drowsily yet dauntingly, from his bed. If only he knew how wrong his approach was, how he was firing my ardor for chair mending, not quenching it (metaphors to honor Tom).

"Where do you suppose," asked I, "I could get one of those huge two-wheeled barrows that I could pull or push through town, to collect the chairs on? It should trundle."

"Oh, Lord!" cried Adam despairingly.

When I got back from the nursery and was planting the cane seedlings, I heard my son on the phone to his older sister, the philosophical one of the three. He told her, "She's planning to pull a barrow through town, crying, Old chairs to mend, old chairs to mend. I think she's gone mad."

(That's what Jacky said they would say of me.)

"What'll we do?" he went on. "It's so embarrassing. Also, the crooked man will find her now for sure."

(I couldn't help but note that the chance of his mother's being discovered and killed was of secondary importance to the embarrassment potential of her mending chairs, but that's how kids are and I don't blame them. When I was young, I would much rather my mother died a horrible death than embarrass me in front of my friends.)

I expected Alice would answer him with some philosophical, tolerant, and consoling remark, but instead she must have said something about my nemesis, Dominic, for Adam next said, "How much money do you suppose she took from him—her 'due,' as she calls it?" This last he said with what I can only describe as a horse laugh—which nettled me, to say the least. If he was going to take Joel's view of the matter, and consider his own mother a robber, I certainly wouldn't lean on him for help and advice, that was certain!

"If only she'd invested some. I think she's pretty broke now."

I had in fact invested some of it in a robotics firm (under Tom's name), but it would be years before I was a millionaire from that canny move, and there was no sense in telling the kids and letting them hope that they needn't support me in my old age after all. Meanwhile I was so excited about my chair business—chair farm, really—that I could think of nothing else.

As soon as Adam was off the phone, I called Tom (home at last from his Mexican holiday) at the firehouse to tell him I'd just planted my first field of chairs and that we'd soon be rich. By chance, he was just back from a six-alarm fire at the Concordia Argonaut Club in San Francisco, and he was absolutely elated, the adrenaline still rushing around like crazy. It had been terribly dangerous and he was high as a kite. "You are the most beautiful woman in the world," quoth he. "There is no one like you anywhere on the planet."

This was adrenaline talking. Still, I was dizzy with delight. It was just what I needed to hear after my son's discouraging air.

"But I mustn't linger," said I to Tom, all business. "You will be wanting your shower and I must go out and mind the cane. I've got a horn, just like Little Boy Blue, which I can blow in case the sheep get in, or the slugs."

"I want you to get a crook too, like Little Bo-Peep. You'd look so cute with a crook."

"No, sweetheart," I said enigmatically, since he didn't know about Dominic at all. "I've gone that route."

I went out to my infant canebrake and sat down in the sun with my horn.

So this is working, I thought.

nine

In the essay "Finding a Career Through Mother Goose," Miliana did not delve into her past so much as take flight of fancy into the future, a foray into possible prosperity.

In her real ongoing life, however, she did not decide to go ahead with it, did not actually plant a field of chair seedlings. She did toss the idea around with Adam just for fun, and the piece contained his true reactions. The phone conversation with his sister revealing his knowledge of Dominic was also true, as was her phone conversation with Tom at the firehouse, for he had at last returned from the wilder shores of Baja California, looking tawny and handsome. She saw him that Sunday.

Tom was a large man in his late thirties, who was beginning to develop a layer of fat over his musculature, which made him even larger, especially over the muscular system of his stomach. He was not one of those big men who are surprisingly graceful. He was one of those big, stolid, graceless men who, when called upon, can move with dazzling speed and efficiency. His physical presence disguised his body's innate strength and talent, just as his rather cherubic countenance masked a sharp mind and wit. He had beautiful brown eyes with eyelashes so long and curly that (he said) he trimmed them regularly so as to keep a macho image. It was hard to say why he was so irresistible to women, but he was and he gloried in it. He was adorable. And he was sexy. Miliana, whose experience with men was not insignificant, realized that he was in fact nothing special as a lover, neither passionate nor inventive, and yet there was no one in the world she would rather lie with. These things are mysterious.

On this first Sunday after his return, and his first day free from the firehouse, they sat together in front of the fog, drinking tequila out of a tiny terra-cotta cup that came on top of the bottle he'd brought her from Mexico, bracketing each shot with a lick of salt and a bite of lime. He questioned her closely regarding all her doings in his absence, as he was always deeply interested in her smallest movements. He wanted to know how Joel was, Soo Yung, Adam, and any news of her other children.

She enjoyed recounting her experiences but of course was selective. She did not tell about the menace in the salon, that being too vague and subliminal. She did not tell about ending it with Joel, as she believed he'd feel threatened if she was wholly available to him. But she did fill him in about the neighbor dog and her search for it and she told about Soo Yung's strange new disapproval of her, and about the hot-tub thermostat running rampant. She told about the creative fit Mother Goose had induced in her but didn't offer the essays to Tom to read, since he was not a reader, not even of the morning paper.

As she had never talked to Tom about her life with or after Dominic, she left out any information that might pertain in any way to the "pursuit."

She knew that he knew that she left things out and that he respected her circumspection, but at the same time his mind would try to fill in the unsaid information. He took her for what she was and for what she wanted him to know of her. He would never spy and try to learn more.

But he would ask. As to anything she had done, was doing, or would do, he was uncritical of her. He trusted her. He loved her. She felt that she could go away for a year or five years and return with no explanation and he would open his arms to her with a smile.

Of course, one could get picky and say that all this tolerance only meant he didn't care for her very much, didn't care if she was there or not there, was with him or with another, lived or died, but Miliana never got picky, especially after living with Dominic, who was so much the emotional opposite of Tom that he made her life unendurable. She was an appreciative woman and clearly thought Tom was one in a million.

"I think you are feeling hurt about Soo Yung," he said, after listening for a while.

"No, I don't think so."

"You should have seen your face when you were telling me about her. Pretty quivery. Also, it seems like Joel has hurt you in some way, said some unkind things to you. You think you are so tough, but when it comes to your friends or your children, you're a softy. I know I hurt you by going off to Mexico, and I'm sorry. It seems like you've been in for a pummeling from everyone." He put his big arm around her and held her close.

"I really don't believe people hurt you. You let yourself be hurt. Therefore, if I'm hurt, it's my own fault."

"Still, friends shouldn't let you down."

"But they do, and will. The best one can do is try not to let *them* down, so that a mutual trust can grow. Still, if we have expectations about someone, they're bound to be disappointed, and how can we not have expectations? For instance, I know you have other women. You've never pretended differently. But it doesn't keep me from pretending, or expecting, that you love me best. That's why I felt hurt that you didn't choose me to be with you on your vacation."

"Even though you knew very well you'd hate the long drive down and the camping out. It would have been your idea of hell. And my idea of hell to have you along."

Miliana laughed. "That's true." She kissed him. "Anyhow, there's nothing wrong with feeling hurt. I always recover pretty quickly, and in the meantime I am reminded that I'm human. Well, almost human."

"What about the dog? Have you told your neighbor what happened?"

"No, I haven't. I didn't want to get Joel in trouble, and I certainly didn't want to take the blame myself. I hope to be able to present him with the dog very soon. He has been sighted. I had a call from the dogcatcher I bribed. He almost netted him yesterday morning. He's hot on his trail. Would you look at the hot tub and tell me what you think?"

They went out together and Tom looked at the thermostat and he told her what he thought, which was that it had been sabotaged. "Who would do that?" he asked her wonderingly.

"Why, almost anyone. You know how mad I make people sometimes."

"Mad enough to boil you alive?" He put his arm around her and they walked back inside to the kitchen. Tom began grating Parmesan for a spaghetti *al pesto* he was making. Miliana washed lettuce for the salad. "Max," he asked her, "who's this guy Dominic Racatelli?"

"Dominic?" She said the name as if trying it out for the first time, her tongue foundering on its strangeness.

"Adam told me he was after you."

"Oh."

Darn Adam. Why was he blabbing it all around about Dominic? She'd have to have a talk with the boy. What a shame for Tom to have found out. It was too heavy to handle. Well, she realized sympathetically, probably that was why Adam had talked to Tom. It was too much for him to know about and not share with someone. That's why he called his sister too.

And that's why she hadn't wanted him to read "The Old Women." She was afraid Adam would get just as upset as he obviously had gone ahead and gotten.

"Dominic wouldn't boil me alive," she assured Tom. "He'd shoot me neatly through the heart. But he doesn't know where I am and he'll never find me."

Miliana gave Tom a brief outline of her years with Dominic, how she had come to understand that he was a criminal, her escape from him, her going underground for a time, and then her flight. "Because of the nature of the man, it was impossible to leave him in a normal, civilized way. He owned me. My life was incredibly circumscribed. I could never go anywhere alone. If he had to take a trip without me, I had to wait at the house for his return, and he would call at all hours of the day or night to be sure I was there. In any case, there were men to see that I was. If ever I did go anywhere alone, such as to a dentist appointment, I was chauffeur-driven, and the chauffeur waited."

Miliana searched for the truth. "You must understand that I was a party to this. It was not just Dominic. At first it was thrilling to be loved so much, and I returned the feeling wholeheartedly. I was glad he seemingly so cherished and honored me. I behaved the same way. The concept of lovers being inseparable, one person, seemed the definition of love to me. But it is unhealthy, insane. It became a nightmare. I was losing myself. I was losing my mind. The shock of learning that he was a crook returned me to myself and gave me the strength to leave."

"Now everything about you begins to make more sense. I don't see why you didn't tell me in the first place. Does Joel know?"

"Yes, since it was he who built me the underhill house, which is how we met. I had just left Dominic and was naive enough to want and need to confide my troubles. I soon came to realize that the fewer people who knew my story, the better, if I was to bury my old identity successfully. Soo Yung knows, since I've known her the whole time. I guess subconsciously I wanted Adam to know, or I wouldn't have written it all down. But now I'm afraid he's going to disapprove of me too, like Joel and Soo Yung. I'm sure Adam doesn't like to think of the Mob being after his mom. It's embarrassing to a young man just getting on in the world."

"I still don't see why Dominic would want to kill you."

"His love naturally would flip over to hate, a hatred as intense as the love had been. Also"—Miliana paused and cleared her throat—"I added insult to injury and took rather a lot of his money with me when I went. Not enough to make much of a dent in his fortune, but enough that it probably made him feel doubly burned. No one pulls a fast one on Dominic Racatelli and lives to tell the tale."

"I'm sure you only took what you felt was rightfully yours."

Was there ever a man with greater understanding? He was positively gifted.

With the salad ready and the water on for the pasta, they repaired to the couch again, where they sat quietly for a while. Then Tom said, "But back to the hot tub. Who else have you angered? Didn't you just say that Joel disapproved of you too?"

"Well, Joel's pretty mad at me." It was all coming out now, tequila talking, plus the powerful inducement of a sympathetic ear. "We had a bad fight about the dog and said some unkind things, or he did anyhow."

She still didn't tell Tom about Joel's finding out about Tom or about her ending their relationship, but moved on briskly to: "And there's some woman who wants me out of the way—a girlfriend either of yours or Joel's. I can't tell you what she looks like, since I was blinded at the time." She told him the "menace" story.

"I didn't know you dyed your eyelashes," he said, a little sadly, she thought.

"Hair too. I'm all artifice. But I'm going natural now. Didn't you notice my gray hairs?"

"No."

"You never look at me anyhow," she teased him.

"It gets me too excited if I do."

"Look at me now, then. I'll show you the parts of me that are real."

"I can't." Tom made a great show of averting his eyes. "I'm sitting too close to the window; it might break the glass." ("It" being his cock and its great size and hardness when aroused.) He heard the rustle of clothes.

"Look now. They're quite something, these real parts. You'll be astounded."

Tom looked. She had covered every part of her person except for her teeth, which were indeed astonishingly perfect. Tenderly he touched them with his own, inserted his tongue and, presently, into her body, his cock—after turning the pasta water down to low. That was the kind of man he was. Joel would have let the pot burn, and Dominic? Well, she and Dominic wouldn't be cooking together any sooner than the nursery would sell rush seedlings—i.e., never in a million years—but if by some freak of fate they were, he would have turned the water off and they would have forgone dinner entirely. Their lovemaking was always epic.

Tom's way was best, because afterward (meaning after a cosmic orgasm not unlike the one the baker's man gave the baker) he let her repose on the couch while he finished cooking dinner and served it up. Then it was his turn to talk, and he recounted his adventures in Baja California, delicately hardly mentioning his companion, and Miliana listened with pleasure. After dessert, hot-fudge sundae, he asked her to play the piano for him, which she did for an hour, and then they went to bed.

ten

In his poem "The Raven," Poe tells of the bird appearing on his bust of Pallas on a midnight dreary as he ponders weak and weary over some volume of forgotten lore. The crepuscular bird has appeared for no apparent reason other than to exasperate the poor scholar by saying over and over again, "Nevermore."

Mother Goose's next and final appearance to Miliana (who had never been weak and weary in her entire life until, it seemed, recently—she was not sure why but hoped it was menopause) was at dawn, around six o'clock in the morning after her night with Tom. She was in the kitchen, putting the kettle on. The fog had vanished and the air was clear, rosy, and all atremble with birds of every feather and song.

It was Miliana's fancy that the legendary matriarchal fowl was somewhere in the kitchen, perhaps on top of the refrigerator (Miliana's eyes weren't quite open and she hadn't had her coffee yet), from which summit Mother Goose declaimed, "Furthermore . . ." and disappeared.

Miliana took this utterance to mean that there was more for her to do. She had further to go. Mother Goose was pleased at the beginning she'd made, but it was an ongoing process. Miliana mustn't draw breath. Mother Goose was saying, in effect, Yes, that's all very well and good as far as it goes, but what now? Are you reaching for a conclusion? And, moreover, what if you die in the meantime, which it's getting to look as if you might? Do you feel that your legacy is complete? Well?

Right, Miliana agreed staunchly, although feeling slightly badgered. Well—she squared her shoulders—the first thing to do is to take charge of all these threats against my person. It's hard to be creative in an unsalubrious atmosphere. I've grown accustomed to the omnipresent Dominic danger and can create with it, but all these other niggling evils (being boiled alive), which smack to me of retaliatory action, must be dealt with. I must find this person (or persons) and defuse him, her, or them.

The water was boiling and she poured it over the coffee. Feeling full of energy, she resolved to interview Soo Yung, Joel, and the beauty parlor women on this very day. But first breakfast! She presented herself with a bowl of cereal, blackberries, bananas, and cream, accompanied by a large steaming mug of Medaglio d'Oro coffee. Tom was still sleeping and could forage for himself when he awoke. He had been on the night watch at the firehouse the night before last, and would probably sleep well into the morning.

But even after breakfast, it was still only seven o'clock, too early to defuse anyone, so, fired up by what she took to be Mother Goose's encouraging go-ahead regarding her legacy, she decided to whip off one more essay before adventuring forth to contend with her enemies and show herself that she was in as good form as any old woman in the rhymes, regardless of being beset.

She decided to address herself to the fascinating and elusive question of love and marriage and get to the heart of it once and for all—by way of Mother's Goose's birds.

She called this essay "The Dooming of an Interspecies Marriage."

An interspecies marriage between a speciesist and an incipient alcoholic is doomed, is my interpretation of this nursery rhyme: "Little Jenny Wren / Fell sick upon a time; / In came Robin Redbreast / And brought her cake and wine. / Eat of my cake, Jenny, / Drink well of my wine. / Thank you, Robin, kindly, / You shall be mine.

"Jenny she got well, / And stood upon her feet, / And told Robin plainly / She loved him not a bit. / Robin, being angry / Hopped upon a twig, / Saying, out upon you! fie upon you! / Bold-faced jig!"

During her illness, Jenny Wren said she'd marry Robin Redbreast, but as soon as she was well, she canceled.

Did Jenny say she'd marry Robin just to keep the wine and cake coming, or was she so weak and dispirited that he got her when she was down and she didn't have the strength or heart to say no? Maybe the wine went to her head and she was drunk. I wish I knew what she was sick with. I wish I knew if she'd ever had wine before. It seems odd to bring cake and wine to an ill person, but in those days wine was thought to be quite the restorative and cake marvelously energizing. Still, you'd think that no matter how vulnerable she was feeling at the time, possibly feverish, even delirious, she must have loved Robin *somewhat* to promise herself to him. But then it turns out she loves him not a bit.

Not a bit. That's strong. I like it a lot. Nowadays when lovers and engaged persons break up, they're so busy saying "Let's still be friends" that they hardly get around to saying how intensely they've come to dislike each other. They're so afraid to make an enemy and have the ex-sweetheart go around saying bad things about them, which they're going to do in any case.

Not Jenny. I like you not a bit is even better than I hate you—as if there is nothing even there to hate. Pure indifferent contempt. No wonder Robin flies (or hops) into a rage, saying, Out upon you! This, of course, is pure gibberish. "Out upon you" doesn't mean anything. Then he collects himself enough to change it to Fie upon you! which isn't a big improvement. One would go far to find a milder epithet than "fie."

Then he shows his true colors and calls her a bold-faced jig. "Jig" is an opprobrious term for black person. This shows that Robin Redbreast is, deep down, a racist. Or a speciesist.

Although he has a passion for Jenny, he deplores the fact that she's a wren and not a robin. He thinks robins are better than wrens and that she's lucky to get him.

Robins *are* better than wrens. They're bigger, have beautiful plumage, a joyous warble, are beloved for being harbingers of spring. You can wish upon the first robin you see in the spring and your wish will come true, whereas no amount of wishing on wrens will benefit you.

The wren is a plain, brownish-buffish, sooty-colored bird that can sing a fine song when inclined but is in fact of a nervous, excitable temperament and given to harsh shrieking instead of joyous warbling. That's probably why the wine was such a success with Jenny. It relaxed her, soothed her nerves, made her infinitely sweeter. She was probably stone cold sober, and at her most excitable and harsh, when she told Robin to bug off.

You won't believe that after this really quite unforgivable exchange between the two birds, they still got married. Yes, later in Mother Goose, Robin comes again and says, "O dearest Jenny Wren, if you will but be mine, / You shall feed on cherry pie and drink new currant wine." (Same wooing technique. He knows his bird.) She replies, "Since dearest Bob, I love you well, I take your offer kind; / Cherry pie is very nice, *and so is currant wine*" (italics are mine).

They both sound pretty smarmy here. This is no noble meeting of minds, or of hearts and wings that beat as one. Not by a long shot.

Robins have a passion for cherries, as anyone who has a cherry tree can tell you, but wrens don't. They eat insects and caterpillars. Caterpillar pie would have been right up her alley. But never mind that. We know, and Robin knows, it's the wine she's after. He'd better keep it coming, is all I can say.

But do you think it's a good thing to base a marriage on? Don't you think the fights are going to get worse as Jenny drinks more and more to try to calm herself? I don't think it's good to marry someone who doesn't like you at all, who doesn't even want to be friends, and who's a drunk. She will only sweet-talk you when the wine's at hand, and pretty soon she'll give up the sweet talk entirely.

This is a classic mismatched pair. The species difference only matters because they can't breed. Still, even that could be overcome (as is instanced by our contemporary gay marriages) if their spirits were kindred. But Robin is the hardy, good-old-boy sort of bird, while Jenny is nervous, sensitive, and frail. Robin thinks she loves him and needs him to care for her, but she doesn't at all. In fact, marrying him is going to make her neurasthenia much worse.

Why does he love her so? Well, wrens carry their tails up and robins carry their tails down. This probably fascinated Robin at first. It is often the odd physical trait that initially attracts and drives you mad with desire for possession. Then, before you know it, a fatal bond has been forged. Eventually Robin will come to hate the way she carries her tail more than anything else about her—as being a banner of her unrelenting, inescapable wrenness. Because deep down, remember, Robin doesn't want to marry a wren at all, let alone little Jenny wino Wren.

If only we could stop the wedding. Why, oh, why, are they going ahead with it? I don't know. I'm confounded. It's enough to make me hop into a rage.

It's not so bad for Robin. He'll be pitied by all his friends for being saddled with a drunken wren. But what about poor Jenny? I foresee incompatibility and thwarted motherhood, leading to acute termagantism. She will shriek at Robin and his retorts will get more and more wimpy. "Please, Jenny . . ."

Their friends know that if they tell them not to marry, they'll marry anyhow and never speak to them again. But one friend, the Owl, is not afraid. He forces the lovebirds apart and imprisons them separately, where they individually undergo a course of instruction in Mother Goose nursery rhymes, and Jenny dries out. They both come to their senses and realize that they definitely want to marry birds of their own feather.

Hurray for the Owl. Jenny and Robin are last seen flying high, singing sensationally, their breasts and throats full to bursting with melodic embellishments. Swooping, turning, fluttering, soaring, they raise their voices in an aria to life, love, and freedom, a hymn to sobriety, and a short, contrapuntal piece to affinity.

When Robin hears for the first time the beautiful song that Jenny can sing when so inclined, he almost succumbs again. He remembers how he loved taking care of her when she was sick and he remembers her tail. But luckily he also remembers the endless scenes and the fact that they *never* had any fun together. Even though she looks and sounds pretty now, he tells himself, don't forget she's real sooty and puffy first thing in the morning, and her song when she's not so inclined is not a song at all; it is a scolding.

Meanwhile Jenny has peeled off and is flying away from him. He treads space for a minute, feeling a terrible wrench. Does she deep down want him to follow? No, not a bit. Don't be a fool, take off—take a chance at happiness! He does.

So it is Robin Redbreast and Jenny Wren, free from each other at last. And celebrating to high heaven.

Miliana was crazy about this essay. This essay, she thought, is the real McCoy. This is honest-to-God, down-to-earth, pure intellectual interpretation, with no autobiography about it. There was not a shadow of Dominic, not a ray of Tom or Joel.

She poured herself more coffee and sipped it thoughtfully, looking out at the view, which, shorn of its white veil, knocked her eyes out with the heightened green of the hills. Now, at the tail end of the winter rains, the ground was at its most lush. Soon the rains would stop for six months and the hills would turn mauve, then gold, then white-gold.

But she took in the sights with only half an eye, as she was still reading over her essay in her mind.

She could be saying something here about her split

with Joel. That she and Joel were not suited could have been the motivating force behind it. They became lovers during the building of the underhill house and remained so for six years in an easygoing way that never grew deeper. They never truly nourished each other or became essential to each other. They had a satisfying physical exchange, lots of laughs, and many nice dinners out. She did admire his work and loved to watch his houses take form. But when it came down to anything serious (if anything in life could be said to be serious), they didn't understand each other. You can talk yourself blue in the face to a person who doesn't understand you, and he will never see the light. If you have an affinity with that person, you will not have to talk at all and he will understand you.

Suddenly Miliana longed to share these thoughts with Joel so that all would be clear between them and the hard words of their last exchange could be forgotten. It was now nine o'clock and he should be up at the job on Blithedale Ridge.

eleven

Miliana got dressed in white pants and a purple-and-white-striped shirt. She wrote a note for Tom that said, "Sweetheart, I am going off on a few errands but will be back for lunch. Thank you for the wonderful night. You're the best! Love, Max. P.S. I'm taking your Chevy so as to confound my enemies."

She slipped quietly out of the house, into Tom's car, and motored over to Joel's construction site.

Among his various vehicles, Joel owned a small trailer, which he parked at each job so that he could have a place during the day to take his ease or, as who would know better than Miliana, his nookie. When she arrived, Joel was just coming out of his trailer, buckling on his leather carpenter's belt with all the tools depending from it. "What do *you* want?" he said surlily.

"I want to be friends," she responded reasonably. He didn't stop walking, so she followed him along the dirt road to his Rube Goldberg invention, a thing of ropes and pulleys and wooden slides, which he used to bring materials upslope to the site. As usual, he had chosen a difficult place on which to build a spec house, liking the challenge.

"Joel, I feel bad about what we said to each other the other day. I don't want you to hate me and think cruel things about me. I want you to understand me."

He stopped walking, folded his arms, and looked her in the eye. "Your idea of having someone understand you is for him to adore you unreservedly, never criticize you."

"What's wrong with that?" She smiled tentatively, but she could tell he wasn't going to be led into seeing any humor. "Sounds like a good definition to me," she said.

"No, it isn't a good definition," he said, with the horrible hard tone he had assumed for the occasion. "A person needs to be talked to straight."

"Well . . ."

"That's why you left your husband, right? Your first husband, that is," he added, as if she'd had about seventeen of them. "You couldn't take his criticism. Whenever the going gets tough, you take off, or break it off. Right? You can't stand to hear the truth about yourself."

Miliana flushed. "I didn't come here for a character reading or to listen to cheap psychology."

"You can't stand hearing the truth," he repeated, in case she hadn't caught it the first time around. "How's anything supposed to grow deeper between two people? How are *you* supposed to grow deeper? All you care about in a relationship is sex and food and laughs."

What's wrong with that? she almost said again, forgetting that what he was saying was exactly what she herself had been thinking about their relationship and what she had come to discuss. Instead she murmured modestly, "I'd say I'm a pretty deep person."

"You're the shallowest person I know."

Miliana was damned if she was going to defend herself on this score, but she couldn't help but point out her main accomplishment in life and say, "I've raised three wonderful children."

"On stolen money."

"It was only my—"

"No, Max, it was not your fucking due. You ripped him off."

Miliana was surprised and aghast. Hurt too. "If you thought these terrible things about me, why didn't you say so at the time? Why did you harbor them all these years?" Miliana hated a harborer, Dominic being the prime example of one. Dominic was a harborer extraordinaire. She believed in prompt forgiveness.

"What you do is your business." He shrugged and made as if to walk away. "I don't give a fuck anymore."

"But now you are making it your business to kill me."

"What in hell . . . ?"

"Someone fixed my hot tub to overheat, and not that many people know where I live—or know about the workings of hot tubs."

"That's another thing," he said angrily. "Every time you break up with someone, you decide he's going to try to kill you. You're sick, Max. Sick in the head." He said this over his shoulder, still walking away.

Miliana had restrained herself admirably, but this last insult infuriated her. And to follow it by turning his back and walking away! That was insupportable. Far worse even than harboring. Anger shot through her, setting up a ringing in her ears. No waterfalls this time; pure ringing. She might have been in a belfry. Sick, am I! Shallow! A thief! I'll show him sick and shallow.

She jumped into the Chevy, gunned it back, then forward so that the front bumper was against the trailer. She gave the car more and more gas, the idea being to push the trailer off its site, hopefully off the ridge. It didn't budge at first, but then, after much burning of rubber, it began to move. What luck that she had Tom's big, sturdy Chevy instead of her frail VW bug.

There was a downhill curve in the road ahead, perfect for pushing the trailer over the edge, where there was a considerable drop—not enough to do any real damage but sufficient to require a tow truck.

With all the carillonning in her ears, the roaring of her engine, the wheels spinning on dirt, she didn't hear screams from within the trailer, or hear what Joel was shouting as he ran after her.

She braked the Chevy as the trailer tipped, teetered, and went over, falling on its side. After slipping a few more feet, it settled in among the trees and ground cover, as if having found the perfect campsite.

To Miliana's utter astonishment, the trailer door opened, upward not outward, and a girl crawled out, screaming her head off. Joel bounded down and pulled her out. He half carried her up to the road, and she continued to cling to him, sobbing abundantly although not hurt in the least, as far as Miliana could tell. Despite her tears, it was apparent that the girl was very pretty—in an ordinary way.

So all Joel's walking off and saying mean things had been a lure to draw her away from the trailer, just as a mother bird draws predators from her young, walking off and pretending to be wounded.

Of course, she had birds on the brain because of her essay. And she certainly preferred to think his behavior was mother-bird behavior rather than an expression of his real feelings about her.

Miliana got out of the car and walked over to the two of them. Seeing the girl was the age of her daughters, she couldn't help but feel a little sorry for her, so when she spoke, she was gentle but firm. "I do hope this will discourage you from interfering in my life any further."

The girl looked at her, her jaw agape. Miliana went on: "As for Joel, you can have him. I wish you joy. He works sixteen hours a day and sees you twice a month, usually for a quick one in the trailer."

Sure enough, she saw from this vantage point, it was one of the girls who worked in the beauty salon. On closer inspection, she also resolved herself into the girl with the high-voltage eyes who'd been in Tiburon the night Miliana had dined there with Joel. Of this she wasn't positive. She would like to ask but didn't quite see how she could. It wouldn't jibe with the omniscient role she had played on two occasions with this girl (in the salon, when blinded, and now), nor could any questions be included in the series of severe and intimidating pronouncements that had just rattled off her tongue.

"Those ones in the trailer weren't *that* quick," Joel said to Miliana peevishly.

"I never did anything to her," the girl said to Joel, with an English accent. "She's crazy!"

"I know," Joel said. Simultaneously, he and Miliana started to laugh. They staggered around the road, doubled up, laughing, wiping tears from their eyes.

"They were pretty quick," said Miliana. "Quicker than some."

The girl looked wonderingly at them. "You're *both* crazy," she said, which made them laugh even more. "You told me not to leave the trailer on any account, and the next thing I know . . ."

"I know," said Joel, looking at Miliana, both of them still laughing.

The girl walked away. Far crueler than the accident was the sight of her lover laughing about it with another woman—with the woman who caused it!

"Now look what you've done," Joel said to Miliana, as their laughter gradually subsided.

"That'll show her nobody fools around with Maximiliana Bartha."

"How did you know she was in the trailer?" Joel was full of admiration.

She knew that the tow truck was a small price for him to pay for the story he'd have to tell the guys, which they would retell over the years, thereby adding to the ongoing legend of Joel the builder and his women.

It would spoil it to say that she hadn't known the girl was in the trailer. She might as well add to her own legend while she was at it. So she just smiled enigmatically, turned, and with a smooth motion, got into Tom's car and drove away.

twelve

Nevertheless, thought Miliana as she drove from Joel's building site, a woman who gets hysterical because a trailer she's in tips over the edge of a road and falls gently on its side among the trees, when she's not even hurt, is not a dangerous woman, is not a woman to contend with, is not a woman of any stamina or imagination. She is just your typical pitiful, jealous idiot who wishes she could kill her boyfriend's other woman but wouldn't lift a finger to do so, for fear she'd break a nail. I'm ashamed that, blinded or not, I fell prey to her animosity and allowed myself to be frightened. "I am not now that which I once was." Correction: "I am not now that which I have been." I can't even quote the way I used to when I was that which I have been—whatever that was.

One thing it was was stronger, she thought, not just emotionally but physically, for although a great rush of adrenaline had carried her through the trailer scene, she now felt so tired that it was an effort to use her clutch foot, and to go from the accelerator to the brake was a feat comparable to the Bayonne Bleeder's leap over the candlestick.

Still, she thought cheerily, the "menace" mystery is officially cleared up, and that's a comfort. A major breakthrough. But the "boiled alive" dilemma remains and is increasingly confounding. Could it be Dominic's doing? All along I've felt it wasn't his style, assumed that when he found me, he would confront me, not kill me in any underhanded, sneaky way. But why assume that? Maybe he figures dead is dead and the main thing is to murder me in such a way that it won't point to him. He probably figures that at the moment of giving up the ghost I'll think only of him. He forgets that there are always others who, however briefly the feeling may dominate them, want to kill me too—Joel, for one, who despite our happy exchange of laughter is going to remain furious with me, probably doubly so because I defused his anger and made him laugh and because I lost him his pretty new girlfriend.

I could be doubly mad at him too, if I chose. The nerve of him, railing at me for being unfaithful while all the time this hussy is just a few yards off, bathing away his latest squirt of semen.

Except, she admitted, he wasn't railing at me about infidelity; it was about being shallow, and a thief, and sick in the head to boot.

A spasm of pain passed over Miliana's features like a gust of wind over water, disturbing the surface. It killed her to have Joel think those things.

She drew up in front of Soo Yung's gloomy little house, parked, and entered.

Finding her friend in the midst of a lesson, she went to the kitchen and made herself a cup of coffee. A reviving jolt of caffeine was just what was indicated at this point in time. She sat in one chair and put her feet up on the other, taking small, steady sips of the sustaining brew.

The kitchen was admirably clean; no grease spots splattered the walls, the counters were clear, and one could see one's reflection in the stovetop. Miliana glanced up at the shelves to see if Soo Yung alphabetized the boxes and cans. She didn't; they were arranged by size and there were damned few of them. Again, Miliana experienced concern for her friend. It looked like times were tough. She wondered what she could do to ease her lot.

Presently Soo Yung came into the kitchen, greeting her pleasantly enough but with no real warmth. Soo Yung had never been a demonstrative friend, but it did seem to Miliana that she was almost cold these days.

Of course, people, women particularly, got more like themselves as they aged, the good getting better and the bad worse; the cold getting colder. Not that Soo Yung was cold; she was reserved. And just because she didn't act loving didn't mean she was unloving. Did it? Maybe it did. Miliana blithely went on the assumption that Soo Yung loved her, but maybe she didn't. She'd thought Joel loved her, and look!

Miliana took her feet off the chair so Soo Yung could sit at the table. She did so, setting down a teapot and a cup. "Why don't you have a lover?" Miliana was surprised to find herself saying. A lover would juice her up, she thought. She wouldn't be so dry and prickly.

"Because I wish to remain true to my husband's memory." She poured herself some tea and wrapped her twisted fingers around the mug as if the warmth from it might heal them, straighten them. She looked haggard and unhappy.

"Why not be true to yourself? A person needs love, physical affection, touching."

"I know that you are a great exponent of that, Miliana, but I hardly need point out that we are different, you and I. There is a life of the mind, of the soul, if you will, that is every bit as satisfying as"—she had an expression that Miliana's keen eye discerned as distasteful—"sex."

It was worse than she thought. Soo Yung had got religion, or something very like it. That must be why she was so disapproving. Life of the mind and soul indeed— life of the bile and the spleen, more like.

"Well, tell me this, old buddy: Does this spiritual life of yours, for I gather that's what you are referring to, include a sort of asceticism?"

"What do you mean?"

"I'm wondering if you are striving for a deprived existence as part of your philosophy of correct living, or whether times are tough and you are hard up for money."

There was a vase in the middle of the table, with no flower in it. What could be more symbolic of Soo Yung's life-style? No vase would be one thing, but the empty vase could remind her to feel resentful. And yet one could always find something for a vase. A dandelion, dried grasses, leaves, pebbles. She thought of her own place, with its profusion of flowers, books, views, the fridge full of food and drink, her lover still snoozing away in the bed of loosened, wrinkled, stained, and body-scented covers.

Meanwhile Soo Yung was saying, "Why do you ask me that?"

"For the plain reason one asks anything: to find out, to know." Miliana tried to keep the exasperation from her voice and failed. "If you're hard up, I'll lend you some money. I'll sell something."

"I am not striving for a deprived existence," she quoted Miliana. "At the same time, I certainly don't believe in self-indulgence."

The implication being that self-indulgence was the foundation of Miliana's belief system, the bedrock.

Miliana wanted to say, Why are you being like this? Please tell me what's the matter.

But Miliana wasn't good at "talking straight," to borrow Joel's phrase. Talking straight was not easy for her to do at the best of times, with the easiest of friends, and Soo Yung was being so unavailable that Miliana knew she could count on no response more illuminating than "What do you mean?" or "Why do you ask me that?" so instead she dropped the whole business and regaled her with the tale of pushing Joel's trailer over the edge of the road, down the brushy slope, and was glad to see Soo Yung laugh.

Half the fun of living, for Miliana, had been to tell Soo Yung about her adventures and see her laugh. However, she realized she was editing the tale of today's adventure, not saying the things Joel said that had made her so mad. Why? For fear Soo Yung's whole countenance would light up in recognition of his censure, that's why. For fear she would shriek delightedly, "He's right! He's right! You are shallow. You are a thief!"

But so what if Soo Yung did agree with him? Since when did she care what people thought? Since now. Joel had hurt her extremely. She did not want Soo Yung to hurt her too. At least not on the same day, within the same hour, when she hadn't had a chance to integrate Joel's abuse and convince herself there was no truth to anything he said.

So she just told the story in such a way as to make Soo Yung laugh. In the end, too, she had made Joel laugh. Maybe by making people laugh she could feel that they loved her no matter what.

More cheap psychology.

But Joel didn't understand her. That had been the original purpose of her visit, to explain to him their lack of affinity and why that inevitably had to lead to their split. Instead of telling him this, she'd pushed his trailer off the road.

Miliana sighed. Maybe she *was* "sick."

"What were these insults he flung at you?" Soo Yung wanted to know.

In spite of herself, Miliana released one of them. "Mainly that I'm a thief. He's got it into his head, after all these years, that I stole that money from Dominic."

"That's ridiculous. You are the most honest woman I ever knew. You'd drive ten miles to return the wrong change. I've seen you do it. Doesn't he remember that's why you left Dominic—because you couldn't brook his dishonesty? But you were decent enough not to take him to court. And courageous enough to take the money, knowing he'd come after you for it."

Miliana felt such a rush of gratitude she about fell off the chair. Soo Yung understands, she thought happily. I was just imagining this oddness in her. So relieved was she that she revealed more of their fight, more of his abuse. "And then he said that I was sick in the head because of my belief that Dominic wants to kill me. Sick!"

Soo Yung's whole countenance lit up. Miliana hadn't seen her look so pleased in a long time. It was as if someone had promised her an even more rigorous life that she could feel resentful about, one with shackles. True, she did not delightedly shriek, "He's right! He's right!" but her voice did warm with pleasure and relief, practically taking on a lilt as she said, "I'm really glad he said that, because that's what I have come to believe. Miliana, Dominic does not want to kill you. He may want to find you but not to kill you. I do not believe he wants you dead. No. I think it is time for you to give up this fantasy that has come to control your life."

Miliana was utterly stunned. She could not believe her ears. If she did have any bedrock to her belief system, it was that Dominic was after her life. For her best friend to tell her that she did not any longer believe this to be true was like Tom being told fire did not burn, or her telling Soo Yung there's no Mozart, which is what she said. "There's no Mozart."

"What?"

She got to her feet, gathered up her purse. "There's no Mozart," she said. "He never lived, never composed, particularly not the Sinfonia Concertante. Mozart is a figment of your imagination."

"I don't understand." Soo Yung was befuddled, but only for a moment. "Oh, yes, I do. But you will see that I am right. You will see. Still, even though I'm truly not worried about Dominic, I'd watch out for Joel. And for his girlfriend. Miliana, I urge you to be careful."

When Miliana got home, her house was on fire.

thirteen

*H*er house was on fire. It was a little like that day she'd returned to her car to find the top down. The top should not be down, could not be down, because she had left the car with it up. Surely her eyes were not getting the correct message to her brain. There was a warp in the synapses. Yes, it was a little like that day but not very like, because that day she'd felt only puzzlement, perhaps some creepiness. This day she felt absolute terror.

Her house should not be on fire, but it was, and her car was still there, which meant that Tom had not left. He was nowhere to be seen, not standing outside with the growing assembly of gawkers, and it was her bedroom, where Tom lay sleeping, that was ablaze.

Miliana took all this in as she parked and leapt from the car. A neighbor from two houses up the highway was standing there with the others. "I've called in the alarm," he said self-importantly. They began to hear the thin corroborating wail of sirens, coming down from the firehouse on the mountain and up from the public safety building in the town.

She grabbed hold of the man's arm. "My friend, Tom? Have you seen him? Did he come out of the house?"

"No, I—"

Miliana didn't stand around to hear any more. She ran toward the house, feeling the heat from the flames, hearing the hissing crackling snapping noise of burning, which is not like any other sound under the sun. The bedroom's outside door was unassailable. The flames had shattered the windows, through which they reached out for more to burn and, finding nothing, disappeared into the shimmering, smoke-laden air.

Miliana ran to the front door. The living room was opaque with smoke, as if the fog had finally burst the barrier of view and window and entered her home—except that fog was fresh and moist and natural, and this was monstrous, a nightmare of acrid, unbreathable, eye-stinging, impalpable poison.

She remembered Tom explaining to her about crawling on the floor to find oxygen and now followed his instruction. She flattened herself and slithered toward the bedroom. She couldn't see, but she didn't need to. The terrain was familiar although she'd never covered it from quite this angle. If Tom was there on the bed, he'd be unconscious. Would she be able to carry him? No. But she could drag him. Somehow she would find the strength. She was a big, strong woman and she knew the marvels of adrenaline. She'd have him out in a jiffy.

Tom was not there. He'd awakened, found Miliana's note, and, it being such a lovely morning, decided to walk on the mountain. Now he returned from his hike, his steps hastened by the smoke he'd seen ahead and then the sound of sirens. Miliana had just entered the house, belly down. He saw his Chevy was there but no Max. The man who had called in the alarm and was so proud of himself about it told him Miliana had just gone into the house, looking for him.

Tom flew. The alarm-caller was amazed to see this

big, cherubic man catapult himself into the air and reach the house in a single bound.

"Max!" he called. "Where are you?"

She heard him. She was in the bedroom now, only as far in as she could get, for the walls and ceiling were aflame. She had made it to the end of the bed, frantically feeling with her hands to see if Tom still lay upon it. She felt sure he was not there, but by now she was dizzy and confused. She could not seem to remember which way was out. She could not seem to remember how to breathe. Nor did she want to. It hurt her to do so. Then she heard Tom call her name and it cleared her mind, even her lungs. She said to herself, Retreat, retreat, get out while you can. She turned. Was the door this way? She lay on her stomach, not moving at all. Crawl! she commanded herself. She obeyed.

Something fell on her face and shoulder. At first she just felt stunned from the blow. Then she began to burn.

She screamed. "Tom!" The pain was unbelievable. "Help!" It was unendurable. She screamed again but this time formed no word. The pain having rid her of her intelligence, personality, and humanity, her cry was an animal howl of agony and terror. Tom had heard such a cry before. Many times. And would again. But because this was Max and the voice still recognizably hers, it would reverberate inside him for the rest of his life.

Miliana wrote this essay in the hospital: "Infirmity in Nursery Rhymes."

In deference to my son, and being in mortal fear of the crooked man, I did not go through town crying, Old chairs to mend, old chairs to mend, but instead put an ad in the local paper. The chair farm flourished. Soon I was able to hire others to mind the cane, the willow, and the rushes, while I tended to the mending and making of chairs, which in due time I could afford an increased labor force to do, so that I could return to my former cherished indolence (my fiddling). I became overseer until I hired one of those too, and then I had nothing at all to do but oversee the overseer and, as Soo Yung would have it, indulge myself to the hilt with, as Joel would have it, food and sex and jokes, paying especial attention to not letting any relationship, or myself, deepen, so that I could maintain my unassailable position of being the shallowest person Joel knows.

The overseer made all the minor decisions, I the major, but there were no major decisions. A major decision would constitute something like whether or not to go to war with another chair farm, or to engage in some small skirmishes with upholsterers. That sort of thing simply never came up. My biggest decision was how far to let the rampantly growing canebrake encroach on my neighbors' property. I said, "Just until it hits their houses." The overseer disagreed, but as I said, he had no say.

It was quite some time before I could find another person, beside myself, who could cane. One day an old Chinese man came to me. He'd been taught caning as a child in Canton. He was blind, but it didn't matter; his fingers knew the way.

"There was a man in our town and he was wondrous wise. / He jumped into a bramble bush and scratched out both his eyes. / And when he saw his eyes were out, with all his might and main, / He jumped into another bush and scratched them in again."

Isn't it wonderful that he *saw* his eyes were out? This was written before cataract surgery was even a gleam in an M.D.'s eye, and yet it describes it to a T, since, in order to make blind men see, the cataract is taken off the eye, which a bramble bush may well have done by chance.

There are no Chinese in nursery rhymes, no exotics at all. And, despite all the old people, few who are infirm.

"Old woman, old woman, shall we go a-shearing? / Speak a little louder, sir, I'm very thick o' hearing."

My Tom is thick o' hearing too. It is not uncommon for firemen to be deaf (or to have hearing reduction, as Tom prefers to say), because of their close contact with sirens.

You'd think that being with a deaf person, I'd constantly bear in mind his hearing problem, but I never remember he's hearing-reduced until he says, "Pardon me?" and then it all comes flooding back to me that he's thick o' hearing.

I myself am thick o' seeing. I was ten years old before anyone realized I was incredibly myopic. I myself couldn't tell. I thought the world was *supposed* to look blurry, no edges on anything, all running together like reflections in water. My report cards read: Miliana does nothing but daydream out the window. I daydreamed out the window because I couldn't see the blackboard or the teacher. Now I am grateful to my myopia for giving me the gift of daydreaming, which has lasted me all my life. Whenever the going gets rough, I can take a trip in my mind, even without a window. As it is, looking back on my colorful history, I can't tell what happened and what I dreamed. For me, reality and imagination are almost one. The line between them was not sharpened by my corrective lenses, so even though the physical world has been made clear to me, my internal world is as blurry as if I never got to see that I didn't see. I believe I still miss a lot. Maybe because I was almost blind my first ten years, I never *learned* to see. It is only since being pursued by the crooked man that I have learned to look sharp, to be alert and on my toes. Now I don't miss a trick. Aside from poor sight, I've been in exceptionally ruddy good health all my life, my only acquaintance with hospitals or pain being because of the birth of my babies.

Until now . . .

Labor pain is a joyous, life-giving pain. I entered into every labor with a high heart and no fear. I gloried in every spasm that just pushed that dear child closer to the air, the light, the life. This is where the phrase labor of love must have originated.

But this pain, from the fire that burned me . . . There are moments when I say to Tom, who has never left my side, "Kill me."

"Pardon me?" he says.

"Tom, I can't stand it."

"Yes you can, Max. Be a man! Be an American! This is war!"

Where was I? Oh, yes . . . Infirmity in Mother Goose. Adam has urged me to write on with my essays. He thinks it will help me through this horrible, horrible time. So that is what I am doing. I am hoping that Mother Goose will instruct me as to how to deal with this pain.

"The girl in the lane / That couldn't speak plain / Cried gobble, gobble, gobble."

This girl could have been gobbling because she was in my kind of pain, but more likely she was so thick o' hearing when she was born that she never heard how to speak and her gobbling didn't have anything at all to do with traumatic injury.

That is the typical sort of infirmity rhyme. Although there's death galore in nursery rhymes, and endless whippings, beatings, and blows, rare is the infirmity and the sickness only occasional.

"As I was going to sell my eggs / I met a man with bandy legs. / Bandy legs and crooked toes. / I tripped up his heels and he fell on his nose."

Almost everyone has crooked toes. Seldom, alas, does one see ten perfect toes on a body. How I wish people in general were more physically splendid. Bowleggedness (which is what bandy means) is pretty common too. His nose, now, is probably deformed by his falling on it, but he's nowhere near as badly off as the maid hanging up her clothes whose nose got nipped off entirely by one of the ubiquitous blackbirds to be baked in a pie for the king.

And then what?

Yes, Adam encouraged me to write on with my essays, but I didn't take his advice until Tom ordered me to in no uncertain terms, thrusting the paper and pen under my nose to shut me up so I'd quit asking him to kill me. His hearing's getting more reduced all the time. He's going to be one of those maddeningly deaf old men who only hears what he wants to hear—things like Want a blow job?

Tom is sitting beside me now to see that I obey him, except that he has nodded off, poor lamb.

Adam came in a moment ago and lit up when he saw me writing. He crept away without a word. I'd rather he'd stayed, but still, I'm so touched. He is my most ardent fan, this dear child of my loins. He has loved my idiotic legacy from the start.

Well, there's Jack, of Jack and Jill fame. He and Jill went up the hill to fetch a pail of water. Jack fell down and broke his crown. In due course, "He went to bed to mend his head / With vinegar and brown paper."

This sounds more like a cold remedy to me, something you'd lay on your throat, not wrap around your head. I never did hear that Jack got up again. This is obviously that same Jack as Jack Be Nimble, our stumblebum of yore. I mean, it's not easy to fall down while going *up* a hill. It would take *our* Jack to pull that one off. He's probably going to spend the rest of his life in bed now, glad he won't have to shamble about town bumping into things, feeling like the laughingstock. Not that he didn't have the excuse of being a punch-drunk—he did. But it's not the sort of excuse that you're proud of, that redeems your stumble bummery in the minds of the townspeople. Although it should, damn it, because all those blows to the head while in the ring during his life as a second-rate prizefighter left Jack with a slow, unsteady gait, tremors in his hands, facial tics, hesitant speech (really hesitant), and pretty much of a dulled mentality. He never was smart or coordinated to begin with, but his mother wanted so much for him to be an athlete (you remember the whole candlestick episode) that he just did the only sport he could, which was to go into a ring and get punched around. When Jill asked him to go up the hill with her, he knew he was in for it. He had a problem navigating the flats—even a bump in the road was a fearful proposition—and she was talking *hill!* But his mind was so dulled, his speech so hesitant, that he was unable to say no in time, and before he knew it, she'd put the bucket in his hand and started off. Now his crown is broken and he's down for the count. Poor son of a bitch.

Oh, Mother Goose, it's hard to write just now. Hard. I'm going to call it a day, having revealed nothing about infirmity, pain, or death, mine as I might through your pages.

But tell me, Mother, would it be unrealistic of me to hope that I need not die a violent death after all, that this near escape can count as the one that was lying in wait for me and now I can just grow old and die like anybody else?

I know it sounds like I'm throwing in the sponge, but I think I would like to live on with Tom, growing old together, neither of us getting more blind or more deaf, neither growing goofy and gobbly. We won't break our hips, as old people are said to do, or break, like young punch-drunks, our crowns. May I hope, too, that a fire won't get Tom as it almost did me, and that one night, or twilight, the sky all rosy, we'll come home from our mountain walk, two good old people, sit down on the couch before the window, wrap up in each other's arms, and die together, I having already talked earlier that day with my three children and he, it's only fair, to his old sweethearts?

I think that's realistic, don't you? Maybe not. Maybe it's one of my daydreams with or without a window. Maybe it's a trip I took when the going got rough. It's rough now, really rough, Mummy Goose, and I'm being such a baby.

But if I can dream of that nice death with Tom, then I won't want to die now to escape the pain. Not that Tom would let me; he never leaves my side.

I hope . . . I hope that Jill's still sitting by Jack.

fourteen

Miliana, near death from smoke inhalation, was dispatched by ambulance to the emergency room at Marin General Hospital, where she was given oxygen and intravenous line. When she was resuscitated, a call was put in to the Burn Unit at St. Francis Memorial Hospital in San Francisco, and she was taken there directly.

She had third-degree burns on her left shoulder, neck, and face, luckily not on her mouth or eye. Third degree means the skin is charred down to the third level of epidermis, so that there is no skin left and skin grafts are required.

She was in the hospital nearly a month. The burns had to be cleaned and debrided. Debridement is the surgical removal of foreign matter and dead tissue. Infection must be kept at bay and it was. Her tissue was in good shape. The skin grafts, taken from buttock and, for the face, scalp, were done in stages of three separate operations, as the blood supply returned to a given wound and it became ready.

She was a woman of strong mind and body, but her body, needing every ounce of energy to heal itself, became weak and emaciated and her spirit became depressed although not suicidal, as in the case of many of her fellows in the unit. Her pleas to Tom to kill her were in passing moments of pain or despair, momentary mental lapses that did not become ingrained in her psyche.

Whenever she experienced these moments of despair she unconsciously began nodding her head in a rhythmical way, so that Tom knew what she was feeling before she said it.

Except for Tom and Adam, she didn't receive visitors until the third week. Both her daughters wanted to come and be by her side, but she said no and was firm. In any case, they couldn't afford the flights. As it was, phone bills were astronomical, although peanuts compared to what her medical and hospital bills would be.

Miliana was in a financial pickle. Did she have health insurance? No. Not if she was to remain off ledgers and out of computers. She did have fire insurance (the house being in Adam's name), but once she rebuilt the burned parts, she still would have to sell the house in order to pay her medical and hospital bills and keep on living.

Her Georgia O'Keeffe had burned too. She did not know if the insurance would cover that. Although her legacy had burned, Adam, with his photographic memory, had recovered it for her and typed it up. Happily, her piano had not burned, or her library. The living room and kitchen and second bedroom remained unscathed from the fire and were only slightly scathed by the firemen.

It was arson. Already an insurance investigator, Don Bradley, had come to ask her if she had any enemies (ho ho).

He was a small, thin, professorial young man with pale blue eyes that did not leave her bandaged face the whole time they talked. He was from New Zealand, he told her, where, indeed, he had been a professor of history. He'd come to the U.S. to visit his sister and stayed. Unable to find university work, he'd taken this job and liked it. She came to think of him as the Polynesian Investigator.

"Enemies? Me?"

"The amazing thing," said Bradley, with some asperity, she thought, as if he were correcting her paper, "is that you don't seem to exist."

At this, Miliana came all over Argentinian, lapsing frequently into Spanish (which she actually felt most comfortable in these days), and claimed she'd only recently come to this country.

"Nonsense," was his response to this gambit. He folded his arms and his glance grew more penetrating. "I've talked to your son, and to your friend Tom Flynn, and to your *other* friend, Joel Jarnding. I can't get any information at all from any of them. I've never encountered anything quite like it. Don't you think it's strange that they aren't more helpful, considering that you've been so badly hurt?"

"Hurt? Me?"

"Don't you want to find the person who did this?" he inquired peckishly.

"Yes, I do."

"Finally, Tom Flynn begrudgingly admitted to me that someone had sabotaged your hot tub recently. I'd say that shows the same sort of mentality as the person who torched your bedroom. But your neighbors say that the only visitors you ever have and therefore the only people who know your habits are your son, your two male friends, and Soo Yung Fong, a Chinese woman whom I will interview later today."

"It certainly is mysterious," Miliana allowed.

"So, I might add, are you. I find it quite curious the house is in your son's name."

"It's not in the least curious. If I die, he won't have to pay inheritance taxes. What's curious about that? Nothing. I almost did die too."

"Would you please tell me about your movements the day of the fire?"

"Well, I'm pretty regular. I had one in the morning. It was firm, about five inches long."

Bradley looked confused, then horribly shocked.

These Polynesian investigators don't appreciate scatology, Miliana thought despondently.

"All right, take it easy," she said. "I spent the morning seeing all my friends. I woke up with my friend Tom, then went to see my friend Joel at his building site, where I imagine he remained until lunchtime."

Bradley interrupted her. "Joel did not remain at the building site. He went to call a tow truck. Although he normally has a phone at the building site, it was in the trailer, which had gone, for some reason, over the edge of the road, yanking the wires out as it went."

"Okay, so he didn't remain there, he went and made a phone call. So what? So the hell what?"

He was not a gentle questioner, more like an interrogator or inquisitor. She felt more perpetrator than victim and as if she were in the dock instead of in bed.

"Mr. Jarnding declined to explain the accident to his trailer. Do you know why or how his trailer fell?"

"I don't see what that could possibly have to do with the fire."

"I need to know *everything.*"

Although somewhat startled at his intensity, Miliana ignored this need of his to know all and continued with her movements. "After I left Joel, I went to visit Soo Yung. She was finishing up a music lesson. We had coffee together. She's my oldest friend and loves me. Joel loves me too. As does Tom. None of them would ever set fire to my house."

"Most murders occur among family and friends. This fire could well have been an attempt on your life. Your car was there, which could lead someone to believe that you were."

"All my friends knew I wasn't in the house. I left Tom a note, and as I had just seen Joel and Soo Yung, they knew. So it wasn't a murder, it was a house on fire."

Just then, Tom walked in. "Can you tell Mr. Bradley anything about my movements the day of the fire?" she asked, flashing him a V with her fingers.

"About five inches, I'd say. That was in the morning. In the evening . . ."

Don Bradley, flushing, got up. "That will be all for now. I'll be in touch with you." He went out the door, walking stiffly—rather like the little lost neighbor dog used to walk, Miliana thought.

"When are we going to grow up?" Miliana asked Tom.

"You keep inhibiting my maturity," Tom said.

The next day, Soo Yung came to see Miliana. Adam and Tom were at either side of her bed, sharing a bottle of Chardonnay and pretty much making merry despite the circumstances. Soo Yung kissed Miliana on the available part of her face. "I'm glad you are all right. I was very frightened."

This was a passionate statement from Soo Yung. Miliana was grateful and glad, for if, as she had told Bradley, she knew her friend loved her, it wasn't because Soo Yung repeatedly told her so.

Adam and Tom went off to have dinner together, and after she and Soo Yung had chatted a bit, Miliana confided, "I'm leaving the Bay Area for a while. I'm going to the Yucatán. I can't imagine anyplace more out of the way and safe from my enemies. I'm going straight to the airport from the hospital in the dark of night before I'm supposed to be released, since interested parties may have found out when that is to be. The stitches will still be in and I'll look like the Frankenstein monster, but never mind."

"It will be hard for you, being mutilated," Soo Yung said.

"Mutilated?" Miliana replied in the asinine way she had these days of stupidly repeating everything people said, as if she couldn't think up any words of her own, or else was trying to learn English as a new language. "What do you mean, mutilated?"

"Well, even with the skin grafts, you will be horribly scarred," Soo Yung pointed out.

"So what are scars? It will look interesting. Who cares? I'm still me, aren't I? I still have my personality and my mind. At least I hope I have my mind. It's been letting me down a bit. The main thing is not to let my spirit be scarred," she said spiritlessly.

Soo Yung said, "You have always wanted to go to Uxmal and see the Temple of the Magicians." She talked cheerfully, striking a positive note. "I think it is an excellent idea. Rest and recuperation and strengthening of the spirit. But where will you get the money to go on this trip?"

"I shall have Tom sell that robotics stock I bought in his name, and that will keep me going."

"I think you're awfully trusting to do that. He could

have sold it himself at any time. Or what if he refused to sell it now?"

"I am trusting." Miliana smiled. "But I'm not dumb. I have his power of attorney, which means that I can sign his name to checks and documents."

"Maybe that makes him dumb. Didn't you have Dominic's power of attorney, which is how you were able to get the money when you left?"

"Yes, but Tom didn't know about all that until recently. As it is, he likes the arrangement because it means I can pay his bills for him, something he rarely gets around to doing himself. While I'm away, I'll have the house rebuilt and put on the market. When it sells, I'll have enough for my medical bills, with some left over. Then I'll decide how to proceed with my life. Maybe the insurance company will find the subhuman who did it. That guy Bradley seems pretty determined."

"You didn't tell him about Dominic, did you?"

"No. Dominic is my business."

"I didn't say anything either. None of us did. It's absurd to think he would have any connection with this fire, but I was concerned that you might imagine that he did, which would only confuse the investigation."

Miliana was annoyed by these remarks. "I do not *imagine* things about Dominic," she said testily. "I know my man and I know it's not his style."

"Good." Soo Yung patted her hand as if humoring a little child. Miliana felt like slugging her. She closed her eyes, feeling helpless. Soo Yung said goodbye, kissed her again, and departed.

On another day, Joel came. Tom was there at the time. It was the first meeting of the two men. They looked each other over in the impassive way that men do, showing no emotion or curiosity, although a light came to Joel's eye that could be construed as a subdued glare—not really hostile; just a quick involuntary flash that he couldn't help, possibly having to do with Tom's profession more than the fact that he was Miliana's other lover. Tom returned the look through his curly lashes, looking benign, then he considerately wandered off so that Joel and Miliana could visit alone.

Joel didn't seem to want to look at her and wandered around as he spoke. "So, Max, what did you go and get burned for?"

"I wanted to experience pain so that my personality would deepen. Don't you think I'm much less shallow already?"

"I hear you went in there to save the fireman."

"Me, save somebody?" Miliana, looking chagrined, said, "Sorry. I have this problem about idiotically repeating things people say to me."

"Then I hear that one of the firemen saved you?"

"Yes. Actually, it was Tom. He arrived back from his morning stroll and found out I'd gone into the burning house to get him, so he then went in after me. I was on fire at the time. He put me out and got me out. How's your trailer?"

"It's okay." He finally looked at her, and they smiled at each other with their eyes, remembering the trailer going over the edge.

"And the girl?"

"Never mind about the girl." He started to pace around again, saying, "So somebody set this fire, apparently."

"Rumor has it."

He plunged his hands into his pockets and stood still. "Max, I'm sorry about the things I said to you."

"You've just intentionally broken a perfect lifelong record of never apologizing for anything. I'm full of admiration. It makes me dare to improve as well. Maybe we'll *both* get deeper."

Joel scowled.

"All right. Granted your apology wasn't graciously received, but you'd be difficult, too, if you only had half a face. And half a house too, come to think of it."

Back to his pacing. The room was much too small for a man of his energy. "I'm going to rebuild your house for you," he said.

"Of course I'd hire you to do it."

"For free. Then you can use the insurance money for your medical bills."

"That is so nice of you, Joel." Her voice quavered a bit and she stiffened it up. "That's incredibly kind. Thank you, my dear. What a good friend you are. It makes me feel weepy, but I don't dare cry because it will seep into the bandages. Anyhow, I'm too shallow to cry."

"Will you just knock it off about all that shallow stuff."

"Yes, I will. I'll never mention it again."

"You never do cry, come to think of it." He thought a minute, and then he said admiringly, "I've never seen you cry."

Both Tom and Joel like me to be manly, she realized.

Tom came back into the room. "Joel's going to rebuild the house," she told him, "for free!"

"Good man."

Joel shrugged it off. "No big deal. It's my work, isn't it?" Joel shook Tom's hand. "Thank you," he said.

126

"What for?" Tom was bewildered.

"Her life."

"Hell." He grinned. "It's my work."

"I know. But you were off duty and it would have been a chance to get rid of her. Max is almost more trouble than she's worth."

"I like to listen to her play jazz piano."

Joel looked surprised. He'd never heard her play. Miliana was surprised too. She'd always thought Tom listened on sufferance. She felt doubly pleased. Joel was going to rebuild her house and Tom liked her jazz piano. Maybe she'd gotten to be a good player over the years, without noticing her improvement. After all, she'd kept at it, played every day. It was her gift from Dominic. Life was pretty good, all in all.

I'm pretty lucky, she thought. I'm pretty darn lucky, if you ask me, having such wonderful friends and being a talented musician to boot.

Then she had one of her despairing moments and started nodding. It was as if she were no longer aware of their presence.

Joel couldn't stand it and left the room. He said goodbye, but she didn't hear him. Tom sat down beside her and put his hand over hers.

Later that day, she asked her surgeon, Dr. Miyami, a Japanese, not of inscrutable mien but possessor of a warm, gentle, handsome face, "Am I going to be . . . to be . . . ? How am I going to look when all this is over?"

"Not very good."

"Scarred?"

"Yes, scarred."

"But I can have plastic surgery?"

"You are having plastic surgery."

"I mean to beautify the scar."

"I'm sorry, but with skin grafts, though we do the best we can, it will never look normal. It is going to look . . ." They locked eyes in understanding, she thinking "mutilated," he thinking "deformed," then they both nodded and in unison said, euphemistically, "Pretty bad." Miliana kept on nodding and looking into his eyes as if entranced, until finally he squeezed her hand and moved on to the next bed.

Tom wasn't there. He had begun to feel he could sometimes leave her side. So it was quite a while before she stopped nodding.

fifteen

B*ecause everyone was treating her* with such kindness, Miliana tried to maintain her lifelong feeling that she was lucky, but it was hard. Her buoyant spirit had got a kick in the teeth. She was hurt, she was mutilated (thanks, Soo Yung), and she was scared. She felt safe in the hospital, but she was dead set on getting out of the Bay Area as soon as she left the burn center.

"The Yucatán?" said Adam. "Why there?" He was looking good again. When he first had visited his mother in the hospital, he had looked dazed and wounded himself. Now he looked his dashing self, all got up in a maroon-and-blue rugby shirt and faded 501s. How American he is, she thought. How Californian! And to have sprung from the womb of this old Argentinian Jew. What will his life be? I pray I live to see it unfold.

"Why not the Yucatán? Spanish is my native language, and the truth is, I'm dying to speak only it. I'm regressing to my childhood. The peso exchange for dollars is excellent right now, so it will be inexpensive. Those are two good reasons, and another is that there is that about a jungle that seems hidden and safe."

I'm scared, Adam, she wanted to say, but she didn't. She couldn't.

She didn't want Adam to remember her as all mutilated and craven.

"Mom." He reached for her hand. "What if you just returned the money to Dominic?"

"Even if I had the money I would not return it, because it is mine, not his," she replied huffily. "And in any case, he is after me because I left him and because I took it, not because he hopes to get it back. I dared to go up against him and succeeded. No one else ever dared to disagree with him or look at him sideways, let alone flout him as I did."

Miliana felt a surge of her old pride in herself, the feeling of being an adventurer rather than this degrading sense of being a victim. "I have always wanted to see the Mayan ruins," she said truthfully, "in particular the Temple of the Magicians at Uxmal. A magical pyramid. There I will find the answer."

"To what?"

"Who was the tenth President of the United States? How high is Mont Blanc? What's the best way to make *linguine al pesto?* That sort of thing."

Adam laughed. "Pretty prosaic for the Temple of the Magicians. How about the meaning of life while you're at it?"

"I *know* the meaning of life."

"What is it?" He cocked an eye at her as if to say, This'll be a good one.

She told him, "It's this." She opened her arms to include Adam sitting on the edge of her bed, his hand loosely holding hers, the two of them just being together and talking about this and that. "This moment right now is what life means."

When Adam left, Miliana called Suicide Prevention, not her center but the one in San Francisco.

"I'm calling from the Burn Unit here in town," she said. "I've been burned on my face and shoulder."

The counselor was a young man. "I'm sorry to hear that," he said. "How are you doing?"

"Not very well. I have some bad moments. At first, when the pain was at its worst, I wanted to die, but that was just to stop the pain. I'm not suicidal."

"What are you feeling?"

"Scared. Of lots of things, but mainly I think I'm scared that I'll never again be what I was. That's funny because I'd been thinking that *before* I got burned. I'd been thinking that I'd lost it. Lost something. I don't know what. My youth, of course. Maybe my health. Or maybe—and this is the bad thing—my spirit. If I lose my spirit, what will I have? What will I be? And now of course I'm going to look different."

"You're going through a very hard time," he said. He was good. "Have you got friends and family around?"

"Yes, I do. They're wonderful. I'm so lucky. I've always been lucky in love."

"That's good. But you're scared nevertheless."

"Yes, I'm scared. That's why I wanted to call. So I could tell somebody that. I don't think I'm scared of anyone or anything; I'm scared of not being able to . . . of not being able."

"What do you think you could do to feel less scared?"

"I'm going to get away by myself, regroup."

"I'd say it's a time to be with your friends. You need the support."

"I know, but I can't find my spirit with them around, because it scares me even more to see myself through their eyes."

"I understand. At least, I think I do."

"Thank you. Goodbye."

Miliana was crying. The tears were seeping into the bandages. Never mind. They'd be coming off today anyhow for good, and they'd be stitching on her new skin. It felt good to cry. She hadn't cried for a long, long time, maybe not since she was a child and lost her mother.

She heard Tom's voice in the hall and stanched her tears. He came in and stood looking at her. He was so kind, so placid, his eyes warm and friendly behind the curling lashes. Like a dog's eyes, she thought. She began to understand that Tom felt for her a devotion such as a dog would feel, one rare among humans, that he would always stand by her and love her, no matter what. Why can't humans be more like dogs? That made her remember the neighbor's dog. I must call the Humane Society, she thought.

"What do you think the meaning of life is, Tom?" she asked.

"Well, it's not original with me, but I've always thought tight pussy, loose shoes, and a warm place to shit sums it up pretty well."

"How charming. Well, after three children, you'll have to go elsewhere for the first." Her heart sank as she remembered that he already did. It was his custom to. Elsewhere was his stomping ground. Would she be able to handle that now? If not, she would just have to leave him. Their understanding from the first had been that marriage was not in the cards for them (anyhow, she was still married to Dominic), and that they would see other people as well as enjoy each other. But now she had broken with Joel and Tom had saved her life and she was feeling terribly attached to him and dependent on him.

She would like to get right inside him and curl up in his tummy and be his fetus. She would like to follow him around like a puppy and sleep on top of his car.

"Tom, while I think of it, I've got to call the pound right now and see if they found that nasty dog."

Tom got the number for her and she talked with the dogcatcher Fred, who said in a tone of humiliation and disgust, "I can't catch the little blighter. I see him everywhere, even in my dreams. But I can't get the net on him. He's quick on his feet. Is he some kind of circus dog? And blimey, the looks he gives me."

"At least he's still alive and okay," she told Tom after the call. "I like that little pooch. He reminds me of myself. As I used to be and hope to be again. Tom, I feel so weak sometimes, like a baby. When you said that about tight pussy and I thought of your other women, it made me sad. The way I feel now, I want to be your only one. I want to grow old and die with you. That's not good, is it? It's lucky I'm going away before you start to hate me."

"Going away? Where? When?"

"Pretty soon. One day you'll come to see me and I'll be gone, having snuck away in the dark of the night. I'm going to the Yucatán, where I will renew myself and find"—she paused and looked self-conscious, because she thought the phrase she was about to utter was so entirely beautiful—*the grace to continue.* Then she smiled and said optimistically, "When I come back, the house will be rebuilt and I can sell it. The Polynesian Investigator will have found the arsonist, and life can begin again."

Tom's face never showed much, but she could sense that he didn't like the idea one bit. "Are you going alone?"

"Yes, I am. You know, Tom, all these years of being

pursued by Dominic have been like a game in a way. It enriched life somehow, heightened my daily experience. And I always felt on top of it and ahead of the game. Now I don't. Now I feel like I'm losing and I don't want to play anymore."

"Why don't you stay with me in the city until you feel strong? Until you can be a man again. The doctor said you'd feel like this, depressed and weak. It's natural. You'll get over it. And I'll lay off the other women until you do. Actually, there haven't been any others for a while. Women these days seem . . . boring. There's nothing to talk about afterward. That didn't use to matter."

Miliana was touched. She could see it wasn't easy for him to tell her he'd been faithful. But she still didn't say she'd broken with Joel. This tenderness between them and need for each other was due to the present situation and would pass. It was not in character for either of them to want to settle down. What they both liked most about each other was their adventurous, independent spirits.

So Miliana responded to his concern blithely and callously. "Thanks for the offer, but I'm off to the Yucatán, and I'll be back when you see me."

Tom got one of those flashes of wanting to kill her—part of the reason, he supposed, that she wasn't boring, but not the good part. He left the room, saying angrily, "You're not in any shape to go to the end of the block, let alone to another country. You might as well go to the moon."

Which gave Miliana an idea for another essay, "The Moon in Mother Goose." Tom gave her the idea, but the moment with Adam when she had realized the meaning of life gave her the substance.

"What's the news of the day, / Good neighbor, I pray? / They say the balloon / Has gone up to the moon."

This small, seemingly insignificant rhyme is a fine example of the meaning of life as I was trying to explain it to Adam, which is passing the time of day with someone you like.

Here you have two old ladies, one fat, one thin, about thirty-two and thirty-five years old, but illustrated in such a way as to look ancient, of course: long hands, bent backs, the whole schmier. They have met on the road— one going to market, the other going fro. They stop to talk. What's the news?

They start off, of course, with the big news about the balloon, the world news. They will go from there to the village news, thence to the neighborhood news, and then at last to the good stuff, the personal news.

This is passing the time of day with your friend.

Soo Yung and I rarely meet on the road, such is the nature of modern life on wheels. Tom and I have *never once* met by chance. What a pleasure it would be if we did! There is nothing more pleasing than running into a friend unexpectedly. One feels an explosion of joy, whether it be off in some far corner of the world or right downtown.

Mostly we have to *plan* to meet our friends, and it's too bad. Everyone's so busy. Their days and nights are scheduled up to the hilt. Except for me and Tom. But even we are busy with each other and turn down every engagement just so we can do nothing together, lie around and look at the fog and make dumb jokes.

"They say the balloon has gone up to the moon." Any news about the moon has fascinated humans since the beginning of time. I'll never forget my exhilaration when man first stepped on it. "They put a man on the moon!"

I said to the first person I saw, who happened to be a black man. "So what?" he said. He had to think the money could have been better spent, but it couldn't have! It was a wonderful, wonderful feat. We have to keep exploring the unknown, even if it means people going hungry, although I don't see how it does mean that. There will always be wars, plagues, injustice, and hunger in the world in any case—as long as there are people who say, So what?

Actually, I realize now how ingenuous I was compared to Mother Goose's neighbor woman. I should have said to the black man, *"They say* we've put a man on the moon," for to this day some people think it was all a mock-up, which *would* have been money poorly spent.

"There was an old woman tossed in a blanket / Seventeen times as high as the moon, / But where she was going no mortal could tell, / For under her arm she carried a broom."

Four people got hold of a blanket, each taking a corner. The old woman lay down in the middle. They picked up the blanket and her with it. Then they tossed her up and down. Once, she bounced, twice, three times, and then she just kept going—up, up, and away!

It's too bad she carried a broom. That's probably how the first witch story got going, culminating in an imaginary air force of hurtling hags on cobweb-seeking devices, fueled by malignancy and venom. Whereas this was a nice old woman, game for a blanket toss, who just kept on going.

She took a broom. "To sweep the cobwebs from the sky / And I'll be with you by and by." She was thick o' seeing and perceived the stars as cobwebs. She had the greatness of heart and incredibly adventurous spirit, added on to her natural housekeeping instinct, to feel that she could go high above the moon and tidy the heavens. It wasn't going to take her very long either. No big deal. This was probably the same woman who later stopped her friend to say, scornfully as it turned out, They say a balloon has gone up to the moon, she herself having gone seventeen times higher, blanket-propelled, having in mind a Herculean task when she got there.

Of course, even seventeen times higher didn't get her there, but it got her close enough to see that they weren't cobwebs by a long shot but zillions of individual planets—time without end, sparkling, glowing, shining, and glimmering off into the unquenchable cosmos.

It took her breath away. It gave her pause. Nothing is what it seems, she thought, as she sallied back down to beautiful, blue-green Mother Earth.

It was hard to proceed with her life after that. She fell into a brown study for a year and a half. Her broom lay idle. Her children ran wild. The experience was too enormous to integrate. Finally, one day, she shook herself all over, and it was business as usual. Life goes on, she decided. Keep your own house swept clean and the children washed and fed and never mind about the above and beyond, the great mysteries. They'll solve themselves in time. One just has to do the best one can and sometimes, in a conversational way, perhaps touch on some of the larger issues.

"They say the balloon has gone up to the moon," she says casually to her friend.

Did they see what I saw? she wonders to herself. How big it all is, how endless? Did they notice how frail our earth is, just a little leaf or petal floating on the deep, dark waters of the universe, which the slightest puff of wind or drop of rain could sink out of sight forever, and . . . and no one would know. . . .

Stop that now, she cautions, giving herself a shake. Don't get started thinking about all that stuff again and get depressed for another year and a half.

She gives her neighbor friend a big warm hug to sustain herself, to feel grounded, which rather surprises the friend, since they're only going different directions on the road to market, not parting forever.

Passing the time of day with your body pressed warmly against another's is a large part of the meaning of life—along with passing it talking.

sixteen

One evening, during visiting hours, Miliana snuck away from the hospital. She decided she would be less noticeable making her getaway in the midst of the welter of visitors than in the dark of night with an alert floor nurse. She'd asked Dr. Miyami several times when she would be allowed to leave, and he had been vague in the extreme. He had been running a series of tests on her that she suspected had nothing to do with her burns.

Her ticket to Mérida was in her purse. Soo Yung, who was the only one in on her secret departure, had brought it to her, along with a duffel bag of clothes, and was now sitting by Miliana's bed as if she were waiting for her to return. Miliana was in the bathroom, where she had gone to change from her nightie to a pair of white slacks and a blue-and-white-striped shirt.

Miliana saw that her normally loose clothes were substantially looser. She'd lost a lot of flesh, a lot of rather nice curves. Viewing her image in the mirror, she thought wryly that she could definitely hire out as a scarecrow. No, strike that: crows would be too easy to scare; try vultures.

It was the first time she'd looked at herself since they'd stitched on the new skin. Talk about ugly. "Mutilated" was too mild a word for how her face looked now. Dr. Miyami had said that at this point her face would look its worst, and he definitely knew what he was talking about. The bandages were off, the stitches still in. The skin graft was currently black and blue and red, and the contours of it, where it was sewn onto her original face, were dented.

As well, it was as if the burn had been a signal flag for her wrinkles to really get going and throw their net across her face. Whereas, before, the lines had been shadowy imprints of character and high feeling, they were now, each one, etched half an inch deep, and what she had laughingly called the dread crosshatchings only a month or so ago were now hard-edged multiplication and addition signs.

Birds are one thing, but I refuse to go around scaring little children, Miliana thought. She tied a silk scarf under her chin, brought the ends around her neck, and tied it in back. This covered the grisliness pretty well. She put on a hat with a brim, which she dipped low over her eyes, then threw on her trench coat, which, not needing it in Mexico, she would check at the airport.

Soo Yung had not said much by way of a farewell, Miliana grumbled to herself as she buttoned her coat. Granted, she'd seen Miliana come and go a dozen times over the years, so it was nothing special, and this time she'd probably be back in a month, but still, still and all, Miliana had never felt so much a fugitive before. She'd have liked an encouraging word, could have used a supportive glance. But no. Stone face. I'd rather be mutilated than stone, Miliana thought, as she gave herself a last look in the mirror and actually managed to compare her own ravaged face favorably to Soo Yung's impeccably smooth one.

She took up her bag and walked briskly down the hall. This tired her so much she was grateful to have to wait for the elevator, chatting casually with another waitee. Presently she was out the main door of the hospital and down the steps. Her idea was to find a coffee shop and phone a taxi to come and get her. Accordingly she walked along the block in the likeliest direction.

It was a pleasant evening, slightly chilly. She was glad of her coat. She looked appreciatively at the stars. She hadn't seen them in a while. And what a long time since she'd seen a sunset! Hospitals should show daily movies of sunsets and starry nights instead of all the infernal television. We'd all get better faster. And movies of moon phases too, she added, smiling and remembering her last Mother Goose piece, about the moon.

Just then two big arms grabbed her from behind. Miliana was not a screamer, but she was in a weakened condition, and if she didn't scream it was only because her heart leapt into her throat and blocked her vocal cords, allowing only a gasp.

It was Tom. At last she had run into him unexpectedly. But she did not feel an explosion of joy. Nor did she say, What's the news of the day, good neighbor, I pray. She glared at him. "What do you think you're doing, scaring the life out of me like that?"

"You feel so thin." He still held her.

"Because I am so thin. Now let me go. I have a plane to catch."

"You were going away without saying goodbye." He looked at her reproachfully.

"I told you I was going to," Miliana defended herself. "I told you one day you'd come and I'd be gone." Then she said, "I'm sorry. It was lousy of me."

"Let me come to the airport with you."

"No, I have to do this alone. I have my ways. I don't

want anyone to know I'm going. You'd draw attention. And people know your car. Come on; you can come with me to the coffee shop. I'm going to call a taxi."

He picked up her bag and walked along with her.

"Thanks," she said. "I'm already exhausted from carrying it out the door. Lord, am I weak! I feel like I've just got out of the hospital. How did you recognize me from behind?"

"I'd know that walk anywhere. Not to mention that trench coat. The world's largest. It's the only trench coat with a train. You should have a little child following behind you, holding it."

"Normally I do."

They laughed.

Who's going to keep me laughing in Mexico? Miliana wondered. Why am I going to Mexico? She suddenly couldn't remember any of the reasons for this precipitate trip. Then they came slowly back: because it's cheap, it's my language, there's that about jungle that's hidden and safe, etc., etc.

"Why Mexico?" Tom asked.

"I'm escaping Mother Goose. I'm afraid she's making these terrible things happen to me just so I can realize a few things and put them in my legacy."

"I don't think a goose could light a match; she could have fanned the flames."

"The Polynesian Investigator thinks someone who loves me did it. That's unacceptable. I'd rather pin it on Mother Goose. People like Mother Goose and God do vicious, unaccountable things. They have their reasons apparently, and they are in a position from which they need not ever defend themselves. Unassailable, you might say. God's will. Mother Goose's will."

"Why does Bradley think it was a friend?"

"Thoreau said, 'I can feel hate for someone I love, for others, only indifference.'"

Tom mulled it over.

"In other words . . ." she started to explain the quote.

"I get it," he said, rather snappishly for Tom. "God knows you're always bragging about how people love you so much they hate you."

"Am I?" It was Miliana's turn to mull. "Yes, I suppose I am."

Then Tom said, as if seeking for a reason to detain her, "The doctor ordered you to keep out of the sun for a year."

"Yes, but that's why Mexico is good. It's so hot I'd protect my skin in any case. Here, I'd sometimes forget to cover up."

They were now in a shop with a phone booth. Miliana called a taxi. Then she and Tom stood in the doorway, waiting. She'd told the cab to pass by the coffee shop and park around the corner, in case anyone had followed her inside and was watching. She'd have to look sharp now, no more gazing at stars. Tom would wait to see that no one darted from the shop after her.

They held hands involuntarily, although ordinarily neither liked a public display of affection. Miliana felt a tightness in her throat and pretended it was still from the surprise of Tom's grabbing her and making her gasp.

"Take care of yourself," she said.

"You too."

The cab drove by and turned the corner.

"I'm going now, sweetheart." She squeezed his hand and started to move away, but he still held her hand. He pulled her into his arms and embraced her. Dropping her bag, she hugged him back. Hard. Oh, his dear, dear body—how good it felt. Tears filled her eyes. She kissed him. Neither spoke. He released her and they looked at each other.

"You're crying, Max. You never cry."

"I do now."

"It makes me sad to see it. Or maybe I'm just sad that you're going."

"Tom, you've been wonderful to me. You saved my life. I love you." She had never said so before.

Nor had he. But he was quick to do so now. "I love you, Max," he said.

Tom watched her walk away down the block. He stayed guarding the entrance of the shop as she had instructed, although he felt silly. What a woman! he thought, looking proudly after her. But why Mexico? he thought sadly. So far. And she didn't say when she'd return or even where in Mexico she was going. It's crazy. And she's so thin. Should I stop her? There's still time.

Startled, he saw a man detach himself from a tree near the end of the block and follow Miliana. By God, she was right!

However, as she'd told Tom, she had her ways. She was immediately aware of being tailed and accordingly disappeared. The man looked around, confused, then started to go the way he guessed she'd gone, which was the wrong way. "Hey!" Tom took off after him. "Hey, you!" But he ran away and Tom lost him. Tom was good at the single bound but not at a sustained run. From the small glimpse he got of him, he thought he looked slightly familiar.

When Tom took off after the slightly familiar man, he was no longer barring the door of the coffee shop, and now another man darted out. He was a short, vital-looking person, with a cheerful expression. He set off after the other three—Miliana, the man following her, and Tom following the man—as if he were joining a parade.

PART II

one

Dominic Racatelli grew up in Pennsylvania, went to all the best schools, and was groomed by his father, a powerful man, to oversee certain operations on the Eastern Seaboard.

He was a dutiful son and honored his father. He was a good businessman, a good family man. He married young and had six children. His father wished he cared more about the business, and about his family, but he didn't. He just went along doing what he had to do as well as he could do it, and was indifferent. One pleasure in his life was his music, but he knew it wasn't in the cards for him to be a jazz pianist, so he never let himself care too much about that either. So he never loved anyone or anything, but as he got older he began at least to acknowledge his dislikes, which included his wife. He divorced her. He didn't like his kids either, or the East Coast, so he moved to California. His father was now dead and he didn't have to be dutiful anymore, not even to his uncles, who had begun slightly to fear him. Dominic was a lot smarter than they were, and *not caring* can make a man strong, because he has nothing he needs to protect.

He was thirty-seven years old when he met Maximiliana Bartha and felt his first overwhelming passion. Seeing her across the room at that reception for Soo Yung Fong dazzled him, hurt his eyes. He fell totally, irreparably in love. He gave her his heart and soul—both of which, it turned out, he had. He revealed his whole self to her. She freed him from his indifference. He came alive. He felt: love, caring, tenderness, joy.

He was thirty-nine years old when Miliana left him, and that was when he felt his second passion, which was to find her. He came even more alive, discovered more emotions: pain, anger, grief, hate. . . .

Despite his lately discovered passionate nature, he was still a good businessman, so, six years earlier when she disappeared without a trace from their home in Malibu, Dominic Racatelli set out in a highly organized way to find her. He knew his woman. She was a woman of the world. She liked good food, good company, art, music, affection, and action. He looked for her in the great capitals and cities of the world, never dreaming she had gone only a few hundred miles up the coast to San Luis Obispo, population 34,252, with no museums, concert halls, theaters, or people she'd want to spend ten minutes with.

A year later, dismayed and confused, also defeated, he'd sought out Soo Yung, to see if he could discover where Miliana was from her best friend. Soo Yung was easily found those days in one concert hall or another, as she was a violinist who played in a well-known quartet.

Soo Yung was a happy woman then, on top of the world. She could afford to greet Dominic graciously. Perhaps she even felt a little sorry for him, as people who are successful, caught in their own conceit, often mistakenly feel toward others. "How are you?" She shook his hand, smiled, gestured to the armchair in her hotel suite. "Would you care for a drink?"

"No." Dominic didn't care to sit down either, and continued to stand, towering over her slight form. He was tall and lean, superbly clothed in a gray pinstripe suit, white shirt, maroon tie. He had thick sleek black hair, the line of which disappeared under his collar, where, Soo Yung knew, it became a dark mat of body hair that, Miliana used to tell her, was sometimes soft and at other times, unaccountably, so wiry it hurt. His mouth and chin were fierce, but his eyes were incredibly soulful.

Perhaps it is hard for eyes that dark not to be soulful, she thought, not to *appear* to be, eyes with heavy lids, that is, for the dark Asian eyes rarely looked soulful. It wasn't a question of Latin temperament, it was a question of lids, Soo Yung decided.

At that moment, Soo Yung's husband, a young up-and-coming conductor, came out of the bedroom. He greeted Dominic, kissed his wife, and departed, saying he would meet her later for dinner. She watched him go, her face frighteningly full of love.

Dominic waited patiently for the door to shut on her husband, and then he came straight to the point. "I have looked for Max for a year. I can't find her. Will you tell me where she is?"

"No." She wrenched her eyes from the door her husband had shut behind him. "No, I can't, Dominic, because I don't know. She has dropped out of sight completely. Even from me. Also, Dominic, I would not tell you if I did know. You might as well understand that now if you don't already. Miliana had her reasons for leaving you, and as her friend, I must respect them. I'm sorry. I know that you love her. It must be very hard for you."

Miliana had told Soo Yung he would come after her, would not rest until he found her, so she'd expected this visit for a long time, wondered at the delay. Perhaps his pride had forbidden him from coming to her until he felt completely discouraged. It must not be easy for Dominic to be a supplicant, although he did not at all give the impression that he was. Even when he said, "You can name your price."

"My price?" Soo Yung didn't understand what he was saying, then it dawned upon her that he was offering her money for the information. "Are you kidding?" She laughed. "You're crazy. Even if I had a price, I would not betray my friend. No, not for anything. Give it up, Dominic. Let her go. It isn't worth the grief. Forget her and go on with your life."

"The offer holds. When you know where she is and want to tell me, I can always be reached at this post office box." He gave her a card with nothing on it but a P.O. box number and a zip code.

"Dominic, what would you do if you did find her? You can't *force* a human being to live with you."

Miliana had said he would kill her, but Soo Yung had disregarded that. Granted, in his grief and hurt he might *want* to kill her; a person might think of doing such a thing, but he wouldn't act on it.

Still, Miliana had said that he was not like other men, that he had his own laws.

So, just to be perfectly clear, Soo Yung tore the card across, put the pieces together, tore it across again, then laid the pieces in an ashtray. "Maybe she'll come back to you of her own accord. When she's ready," Soo Yung said.

She flushed, seeing Dominic's scornful look, and had to ask herself what she would do if her husband left her. Would she wait passively for his return of his own accord?

"There are other ways," he said casually—oh, so casually—so that the import hardly penetrated, "to learn this information. Your hands could be hurt, or your loved one."

She could not give credence to such a remark. She was a woman on top of the world: successful, loved, therefore invulnerable. "Really, Dominic, how melodramatic. I'm embarrassed for you. Now excuse me, but I must dress for dinner. Ciao, Dominic."

Within a year of that interview, she had lost both her husband and her hands. Her loved one had died of a heart attack. Her hands had been struck by rheumatoid arthritis. She *knew* that Dominic had nothing to do with either of these things, that there was no way he could have, and yet the fact remained that he had threatened her with these two things and they had come to pass.

In her memory the threat reverberated and reverberated, gathering force. She began to feel she had made a terrible mistake.

She moved to Mill Valley, into her gloomy rental in the canyon, a grieving, increasingly crippled widow.

Into this same town in due course came her old friend Miliana. Miliana pursued, but Miliana full of life, love, wit, and sensuality. While life's juices had drained from Soo Yung, they had fermented in Miliana. She was like a sparkling wine.

Instead of letting this wine of her old friend animate and cheer her, Soo Yung began to blame Miliana for what had happened to her. It began to seem that because she had not told Dominic where Miliana was, she had lost her husband and music.

Never mind that she hadn't known where Miliana was. Never mind that she hadn't even taken Dominic seriously. Never mind that what transpired could not have been Dominic's doing. It seemed crystal clear to her that she had lost all that was meaningful to her, all that was precious, because her principles had not allowed her to sell out her friend.

And this friend was not worth it, was a lowlife. She began to see Miliana as an immoral woman, one who had never worked, who lived off the money of others, lived for pleasure, made no useful contribution to society. While Soo Yung scrimped and drudged, giving lessons to no-talent brats, Miliana rollicked boisterously along through each day, doing absolutely nothing.

And it was for this woman that Soo Yung had lost everything!

Reading Miliana's Mother Goose essays further inflamed her feelings of resentment. Miliana had no understanding at all of what life was. She had not a serious bone in her body. Her mentality was adolescent. She had no conception of human suffering. Her idea of pain was hearing Tom tell her he was going to Mexico, which meant that for two weeks she'd have only one lover instead of two. Her idea of work was to plant a field of chairs, for heaven's sake, and lie around and watch them grow, blowing a horn to keep off the slugs.

But there was justice after all, because her house caught fire and Miliana was horribly burned. Aha! Soo Yung thought. Now she will see what life really is. Now she will experience it as I have.

Soo Yung, although still bitter and resentful, was prepared to be loving and sympathetic to Miliana in her plight, but when she finally got to go to the hospital to see her, there she was, quaffing wine, cracking jokes, attended by Tom and Adam, sitting there like a queen, her bandages jeweled ornaments, her wineglass a scepter.

When she told Miliana the facts, that she would be mutilated, she didn't care, said it would look interesting, declared she would still be her fabulous self and what did her looks matter. Gaily she planned a trip to Mexico, enlisting Soo Yung's help.

At that moment she could have killed her.

Dominic Racatelli was now forty-five, more human and passionate than ever and hardly attentive to business, so wholly had his search for Max consumed him. He was in Rome when his clipping service forwarded the news about the fire in the house of Adam Jones. Although it was some weeks after the fact, he thought it worth following up, on the slim chance the Adam Jones was Miliana's son. He sent a low man on the totem pole—one Dub, to investigate. In time came a report from Dub, who had suborned the insurance investigator to learn the information Dominic required.

This was the essence of the report: Yes, the house was actually Miliana's, in the name of her son. She lived there alone when she wasn't visited by Adam, by Joel Jarnding, a builder, or by Tom Flynn, a fireman. Her friend Soo Yung Fong lived in the same town. Tails on all these people had taken Dominic's man to St. Francis Memorial Hospital, where he learned that the subject was recuperating from burns. Not due to be released until sometime in April, she left unexpectedly on the evening of March 23. Dub was on the scene at the time, saw her meet Flynn in front of the hospital. He followed them to a coffee shop, where she placed a call. She stood in front of the shop, said farewell to Flynn, and walked away. Waiting for Flynn to move away from the door before following her, he mistimed and lost her.

Dub's report went on to say that the following day he had gone to her damaged house, which was being rebuilt by her builder friend. Joel Jarnding told him Miliana had gone away for an indeterminable amount of time to an unknown place.

"That's it," the report concluded, on a familiar note, for Dub longed to be on a more intimate footing, longed to become invaluable. "Sorry, boss. And I'm really sorry about losing her. I've never been too good a tailer. I got to hone my skills is what. I followed the fireman, thinking he was following her, but he wasn't. He was following another guy who'd been trying to follow Ms. Bartha and went the wrong way. Flynn started yelling at him and the guy took off like a shot. I passed up Flynn and kept after the other guy, who turned out to be Ms. Bartha's neighbor, a guy named Caesar Smith. Now what do you make of that?"

Dominic Racatelli read this report and tightened his lips. Again, Miliana had eluded him.

two

Dominic flew to San Francisco, checked into the Huntington Hotel on Nob Hill, and went to see Soo Yung, with
no advance warning. He simply drove the fifteen miles to
Mill Valley, went to her house, and rang the bell.

Soo Yung didn't recognize him, and he had to tell her
who he was. This time he was not armored in pinstripes
but wore white linen pants and a light blue shirt. His hair
was tousled and the muscles of his face had relaxed. He'd
put on a little weight, was no longer knife-edge lean and
tight.

But he still came straight to the point.

He said, "I will give you twenty-five thousand dollars
right now, in cash, if you will tell me where Max has
gone."

Unhesitatingly, she told him he would find Miliana in
Uxmal.

He was staggered at the simplicity of it. His body
actually rocked back on his feet as if he'd been pushed.
For an instant he almost felt disappointment. Then he
knew it was relief, such enormous relief! Shortly, in a
matter of days, maybe hours, he would be free of Max
and of his search for her, which had dominated his life for
so long.

"I only tell you this," Soo Yung explained, "because
I need the money so desperately now. And because I
know that you only want to find her, not kill her, as she

157

has always pretended. She has dramatized your pursuit of her to the point of nausea. I'm so weary of the whole business, I can no longer stand it. I'm glad to have it all over with at last. And I'm very glad to have the money, which is owed me by her. She is heavily in my debt," she said, believing it, so twisted had her thinking become. It's my due, she thought, and laughed to herself. My due.

"Yes," said Dominic, scrutinizing her. "I see life has been hard for you and you feel cheated and wronged. Perhaps the money will make things easier. I hope so. However, you are wrong about one thing: I *am* going to kill her."

At this point Soo Yung could have done one of three things. She could have denied to herself that she had heard him say it. She could have denied that he meant what he said. Or she could have felt terrible remorse, combined with panic, and warned Miliana at once.

She didn't do the third thing. She did one of the first two; it doesn't matter which.

In no time at all, less than an hour after Dominic's departure, she began to view the twenty-five thousand dollars as compensation money for the loss of her husband, to find it insufficient, and to loathe it. If she was going to take money as reparation, why had she not taken more? This could not buy her a house and could barely buy her a car. It certainly would not buy her the love of a gentle, talented man such as her husband had been. Nor would it straighten her fingers, succor the pain. Miliana herself must have taken hundreds of thousands from Dominic, just as money to go on with, and this was . . . blood money. Her brain winced at the thought. It curled her hair. But it was true. Blood money is compensation paid to the survivor of a slain man. Blood money is also money paid to an informer, but to respond in any way to that definition would be to acknowledge the truth of the transaction just concluded between herself and Dominic. Her denial was so successful on that score that had someone mentioned Miliana's name, she'd have had to think twice to even remember who she was. In fact, just as Miliana had regressed to Spanish during the time of her pain and despair, Soo Yung was at this very minute burrowing back down into the warm cocoon of Chinese, the language she had spoken as a child, before she knew Miliana, before she even knew music.

So when the phone rang, she answered in Chinese, and when Joel Jarnding asked her if she had any address at all for Miliana, she still responded in Chinese, but even so, not with the answer. She just talked singsongy nonsense, something comparable, no doubt, to a Chinese nursery rhyme.

Joel, mystified, concluded that Soo Yung had family visiting. He had wanted to get an address for Miliana so he could call and tell her about the strange man with the cheerful face who had come asking for her whereabouts.

After his unsuccessful exchange with Soo Yung, he got hold of Tom through the fire department, but Tom knew only that she'd gone to the Yucatán, an amorphous jungly area somewhere—God knew where exactly—in Mexico. Adam, when reached, remembered that she was flying to Mérida, then going on to Uxmal, but he didn't know where she was staying. He said Dr. Miyami had freaked out at her leaving the hospital, and they were all supposed to try to get her back.

Joel figured, heck, if no one knew where she was, the

cheerful-faced guy wasn't going to find out either. He regretted that he hadn't asked him a few questions as to who the hell he was and what business it was of his— even worked him over a bit. In the end he figured it was smarter to appear disinterested. He'd just played the laconic builder.

Tom was upset by Joel's call. After thinking about it, he called him back at Miliana's house. "The night Max went to Mexico," he told him, "I ran into her outside the hospital. She wouldn't let me go to the airport with her, but we waited together for a taxicab. As she was walking to the cab, some guy started following her. She realized it and did some maneuver that lost him. I went after him, but he bolted and was too fast for me. But the thing was that he looked familiar. I had the feeling I'd met him somewhere once. Actually, because I'd just met you, I thought it might be you. Was it?"

"No."

"I wonder if it was the same guy who asked you where she was. What did he look like?"

"He was short, sort of a nice-looking guy, cheerful. Funny way of talking."

"No, that wasn't him. This guy I saw was pretty tall and definitely not cheerful."

"I should have asked him who the hell he was," Joel said morosely. "Fuck. I've just been sitting here regretting that I didn't."

"Maybe he's part of the arson investigation," Tom said, with a lift to his voice. "Yeah, that's probably it. Let's go talk to that guy Bradley. The Polynesian Investigator."

They both laughed. Suddenly it seemed as if Miliana were right there with them on the phone line, and it made them warm to each other. Tom told Joel the story of Miliana's "movements" on the day of the fire, and they laughed again.

They arranged to have lunch together in the city the next day, then go see Bradley.

three

The man who sent the report to Dominic was named Dub because his lips weren't in sync with his voice. The investigator he suborned was Bradley.

When Dub bought the information about Max from Don Bradley for two thousand dollars, he told him the truth, which was that her husband was looking for her.

There was nothing alarming in that, Bradley thought. Why shouldn't a husband be able to get in touch with his wife? He'd probably done them both a favor. As for taking the money, suppose he were a private investigator, hired to find this information? He'd take the money, wouldn't he? What was the difference? Now, if Dub had paid him to sabotage his investigation, that would be something else entirely, or to give false information to his insurance company. But no, Dub simply wanted to know where Maximiliana Bartha was and who her friends were.

Bradley wanted to learn everything he could about Maximiliana Bartha. It was clear to him at the start that Miliana was hiding from someone, and his curiosity had been piqued. He was insatiably curious, which was one reason the job so suited him. All his files were bursting with ten times more information than he needed on any case, because his curiosity led him down so many avenues. One thing led to another. There was always more to know. Often, long after a case was closed, he was still, on his own, prying into that person's life. Sometimes he investigated people he was interested in even if they weren't connected with a Miwok Insurance case. It was his great good luck that Miliana, or her son rather, was a client of the company.

He knew it hadn't been a murder attempt, really. He just said that so he could keep asking questions—not that arson wasn't serious enough ground for questions in its own right.

His main reason for selling the information to Dub was in the expectation of learning some facts about Miliana in return. He was disappointed, and although the money proved to be somewhat of a sop to his disappointment, he'd rather have added to his file. Bradley did not like Miliana. Among other reasons, he could not forgive her the joke about her "movements," and it infuriated him further when she included Tom Flynn in the joke, which was essentially against him. It seemed that he could never again use that word in his investigations, and for the life of him he couldn't come up with an alternate word. Motions made no sense. Can you tell me about your motions on the day of the fire? He had already tried that, and the person looked at him sideways.

So what with one thing and another, he felt no twinges of conscience about having taken the money from Dub.

Since he was investigating as vigorously as ever and felt he had not done wrong in taking the money, why then, when the two big men, the fireman and the builder, brazened their way into his office unannounced, did he feel so scared? Why did he wish himself safely ensconced back in the University of Auckland, teaching the history of England and investigating dead people like Henry VIII?

Tom and Joel enjoyed a splendid lunch together at a popular San Francisco restaurant called Le Central. Here, in the business district, they were the only men not in suits and ties, but they both looked sharp: Tom in khakis and a white broadcloth shirt, which was about the dressiest he ever got except for funerals, and Joel in designer corduroy pants, plaid cotton shirt, and dark blue V-neck cashmere sweater. Joel spent a lot of money on his clothes but didn't wear them well—they weren't designed for men with muscles. He looked best in his work clothes.

Neither man was college-educated or even very self-educated, but they spoke well, were smart as the dickens and good at what they did, loved a good laugh, and had straight white teeth to show for it. They were vivid.

It was no surprise to either of them that every woman in the place only had eyes for them, and they had fun dividing them up, imagining scoring with them, and giving their considered opinion of how the lay had been. Men of their erotic experience could pretty well tell at a glance how a woman would be. There was only one woman, a muscular blonde, they were of two opinions about, which made them both want to find out. They flipped and Tom won. As she was leaving, he intercepted her at the door and easily set up a date for the following evening.

When Tom came back to the table, there was a young woman standing belligerently over it. Joel attempted to introduce her, but Tom could tell he didn't remember her name and so saved him by saying, "I'm Tom." He got a relieved look from Joel.

"I've been up to the job, but you're never there," she said to Joel complainingly. "Then I found out you're rebuilding that woman's house. I can't see why you'd want anything to do with her after what she did."

"Max?" interrupted Tom. "What did Max do?"

"Never mind," Joel said.

"I know all about it now," she said. "You've been seeing her for years! You're nothing but a lousy two-timer. It's all over with us, you can be sure of that!"

If only that were true, Joel thought. It's always the ones who say that who keep after you. He made a non-committal noise that he hoped would neither encourage her tirade nor discourage her stated intention.

"I'll bloody well be sending you the medical bills," she said as a parting shot before flouncing away.

"Medical bills?" Tom asked.

"Not an abortion, just a little accident. Do you ever have the problem of not remembering a woman's name?"

"Yeah. It's particularly bad when you've spent the night with her. I saw a girl in Safeway the other day and for the life of me I couldn't remember her name. It was even worse because at first I didn't remember her face either, and I started to make a pass practically in the same words I'd used the first time—which was also in Safeway. These are perilous times."

"You need a new supermarket, guy," Joel said.

Tom raised his glass. "Here's to you, you lousy two-timer."

Joel and Tom discussed the problems inherent in being a lady-killer, and all this good talk was embellished by fine food and several beers, so they were in rollicking good humor when they burst in on Bradley. These were men who might deign to make an appointment in advance with a woman but certainly not with an insurance agent.

Bradley stood up so fast he knocked over his chair. He backed up until the wall prevented him from going any farther. Even the most ebullient eye could see the man was frightened. It was Tom who deduced why. He put on a tough-guy act that any of his firemen friends would have seen through in an instant but which impressed Bradley and even Joel. "You weren't expecting us, were you?" he said, talking through clenched teeth, a trick he had practiced. (Miliana loved it when he talked to her that way.)

Bradley was not without dignity. He pulled himself together, stood straight, squared his shoulders, and said, "You have no appointment. Therefore I was startled."

"You were scared shitless," said Tom.

Even then, Bradley thought about "movements." It was to become the curse of his life.

"Startled?" Tom addressed Joel. "You call that startled when a man practically has a heart attack because we walk in the door?"

"No, I don't," said Joel. "I'd say the man feels bad about something. Real bad."

"Did you tell that little happy-looking guy where Max is?" Tom continued his through-the-teeth interrogation.

"No, I didn't," Bradley responded honestly. "I don't know where she is. Where is she?" (He couldn't help asking; he was dying to know. Just to know. Still, he could have bitten off his tongue.)

"What *did* you tell him?" Joel asked.

"He wanted to know if Adam was the son of Maximiliana Bartha. He'd read about the fire. I said he was. Then he wanted to know who her friends were, and I told him. That was all."

"What did he want to know for?"

"He said her husband was looking for her."

At this, a meaningful look was exchanged between the two men that drove Bradley wild with curiosity. "I figured he needed the information that she was living with a man for divorce proceedings—"

"There's no-fault divorce in this state," said Tom.

"Why did he want to know, then? Which husband was it? Who is she? Why is she so mysterious? She literally doesn't exist. She has no credit cards, no driver's license, no bank account, no—"

"Shut up," Joel said.

"Yeah, shut up," said Tom, through his teeth.

To their amazement, Bradley didn't shut up. He rattled on, a man caught in the grip of a subject that consumed him. His eyes sparkled, his color heightened. His arms and hands made wide, expansive, often elegant gestures. "She says she's just over from Argentina, but she became an American citizen when she married Jones twenty-five years ago."

"Twenty-five years ago?" they repeated. How old *was* she anyhow? They realized Bradley probably could tell them, but it wasn't the sort of thing they could ask him through their teeth.

"She divorced Jones"—Bradley talked on to his now enraptured audience—"when Adam was ten—this sort of thing *is* on record—and married Dominic Racatelli that same year. Jones married again and had four children, three girls and a boy."

Tom and Joel were listening attentively, but they couldn't help wondering what all this had to do with the fire.

"She only lived with Racatelli for two years. She

never divorced him. That's when the big blank begins. For all intents and purposes, she no longer exists. It's possible that she isn't even who she says she is."

"Adam seems pretty confident she's his mother," Tom reminded him.

Bradley blushed. "That's true. I guess I was over-dramatizing."

This confession released Tom and Joel from the spell. It was Joel's turn to get tough. "Why don't you just find out who the hell set the fire, instead of how many kids her ex-husband had, for Christ sake?"

"I fully intend to," said Bradley, drawing himself up huffily.

"What have you discovered so far?" Tom asked in normal tones, feeling it was no longer appropriate to talk through his teeth. Besides, his jaw muscles were tired.

"That neither of you did it."

Again they exchanged glances, never having considered they were under suspicion.

"You, Tom, truly went for a stroll well before the blaze started, and there was no timing device to delay it. Joel has been placed well away from the scene. Miliana had pushed his trailer over the edge of the ridge, and he was engaged in recovering it."

"Max pushed your trailer!" Tom somehow imagined her doing it with her bare hands. "Why?"

"Never mind," Joel said. "It has nothing to do with the fire—just like all the rest of this asshole's information."

"What about Soo Yung?" Tom asked, remembering that Bradley had a "loved ones" theory. "Where was she at the time?"

"I only began looking into her motions recently, but she has unaccountably lapsed into Chinese."

"Motions?" Tom asked, innocently at first. Then he remembered. He and Joel started to laugh.

Bradley flushed, further humiliated to learn that Joel was now in on the joke. "If you gentlemen—I should say children—are satisfied, I have work to do."

"Yeah. I suppose you got to find out if Max's first husband's children brush their teeth at night. Right?"

"And floss," said Tom. "Find out if they floss. That's bound to lead you to the arsonist."

Bradley showed them the door. They obliged by going through it.

As they walked to the Stockton Street Garage, Joel said musingly, "That must have been Dominic's man looking for Max. I don't like it."

"Why do you think Bradley was so scared when we came in?"

"I suppose we did surprise him, bursting in like that."

They walked along, each man thinking. Joel spoke again. "Another thing: there's no way on earth he could have known about Max pushing my trailer over. Max would never tell him. Why should she?"

"She didn't tell me," Tom said, a little sulkily. "But that guy seems to find out everything. He's incredible."

"Yeah, except who lit the fire."

"Why did she push the trailer over?"

"I don't know. Why does Max do anything? I said something that annoyed her. The problem was, there was a girl inside it."

Tom laughed. "Medical Bills? Was that the accident? Now I get it. Well, maybe Medical Bills told him."

"How could he have known about her to ask?"

"Imagine that guy suspecting us," Tom said. "Especially me."

"Luckily, you 'truly went for a stroll.'"

"I've never strolled anywhere in my life." Tom was insulted. "I walk like a *man.* I hike!"

"Not anymore, you don't. Bradley says you stroll, you stroll. He's an authority on motions."

They had a good laugh over that one, paused to part company, and went to their respective vehicles, promising to try to alert Max about Dominic. "Not that she's not constantly on the alert anyhow," said Joel.

"I never even knew about Dominic until recently," Tom said. "She never tells me anything." He was embarrassed to realize it was the second time he'd made such an admission in the space of a few minutes. He guessed he was feeling hurt about Max's keeping secrets from him all the time he thought they were so close.

Joel was pleased. "I know everything about her," he bragged, feeling proud that this was true. "She's always been able to confide in me."

Tom flushed slightly, then mentioned with studied casualness, "That being the case, it's funny you didn't know about her piano playing."

It was Joel's turn to flush.

Tom went on in a bemused tone. "She obviously saves the things that really matter for when she's with me. I could tell you other things too, but, well . . ."

Joel glared at Tom. His fists doubled and his shoulders dropped. Tom straightened, stood chest out, centered, eyeing him back.

But these stances were involuntary and occupied only

170

a few seconds. Their good humor and real pleasure in each other prevailed. They smiled, relaxed, shook hands, and parted, promising to meet again soon.

Meanwhile, back in his office, Bradley was looking over Miliana's phone bills of the month preceding the fire. She made very few calls for a woman: to Tom at his fire station, to Joel at his building site (both of these numbers seldom), to Adam in Berkeley, and two to her daughter in New York. There were several unspecified local calls. The only interesting number was to Oakland, just a week before the fire. In his cross-reference book, he ascertained that the number belonged to the Humane Society. Now that was curious.

By the next afternoon, after showing Miliana's picture to every person who worked there, he had contacted Miliana's particular dogcatcher, Fred. They talked to each other as fellow professionals, Bradley being a fire-starter catcher and therefore in somewhat the same line of work. Needless to say, Bradley could not conceive of the connection between Miliana and an East Bay dog, and was dying for an explanation.

It was a while coming. Fred had become a man with a mission. All he wanted in life was to catch the "little blighter." It was his all-time hardest case. Although he was close to retirement, he would put that off if he had still not caught the animal. He would retire with honor or not retire at all. He had even resorted to a tranquilizer dart gun, used only with dangerous animals, but "talk about a tough hide," the dog was apparently armor-plated—the darts bounced off him. Fred had come to feel the dog was taunting him, that it actually "follows me around and makes a mock of me."

The saga was long, Bradley was patient. At last Fred got to Miliana and the bribe. (A bribe! Bradley's eyes popped with excitement.) How had this dog of Ms. Bartha's got to the East Bay? Bradley asked him.

"A friend drove it over here, maybe just taking it along for the ride, and it got away, was all she said. She was bloody upset about it."

After yesterday's confrontation with Miliana's lovers, Bradley didn't feel inclined to talk to Joel or Tom about the dog so he again tried to get an interview with Soo Yung, and this time he succeeded. He went to her house. She asked him to excuse the disorder. She was packing. She was moving to the Napa Valley.

Bradley's insatiable curiosity wasn't sparked by the fact that Soo Yung was leaving town, because his curiosity was full of the dog development. Also, like many New Zealanders, he wasn't interested in nonwhite people.

Also, he knew Soo Yung had not set the fire.

"Miliana does not own a dog," she informed him.

"I have certain information that she was at the Humane Society, looking for a little brown dog that someone drove over the bridge to Richmond."

"Nonsense. Miliana has never owned a dog of any description, and if for some reason she were looking for one, I'd have known about it. Miliana told me everything . . . *tells* me everything."

"The dogcatcher says a friend of hers drove the dog over and it got away."

"It's the unlikeliest thing I ever heard of. Even if she had a dog, why would a friend give it a ride to Richmond? She doesn't have friends in Richmond. Nobody does. Adam, her son, is in Berkeley, and Richmond is on the way there. It must have been Adam who took this imaginary dog there. Ask him."

"She paid a dogcatcher to make an especial effort to find him—that's how important the dog was to her."

"Miliana's a spendthrift. If she can think of any reason to give someone money, she will. Especially when it's not her money, money she never earned by the sweat of her brow. She has never worked, you know, and therefore has no concept at all of the value—" Soo Yung brought herself up short. She was running off at the mouth, for no reason.

"Whose money did she live on, then?" Bradley asked. "Tom's? Joel's?"

"What has that to do with the fire?" Soo Yung flashed angrily. "For that matter, what has the dog to do with it?"

Bradley called Adam in Berkeley, taking the number from Miliana's phone bill. Adam said he didn't know anything about a little brown dog that someone had driven to Richmond.

four

Miliana, having a drink by the pool of the Hotel Mayaland, tried to think that the creature darting under the
next table was not a rat, but it was too large to be a mouse
and there was that about its tail that forbade its being a
squirrel or a chipmunk, which she doubted were jungle
animals in any case.

Should she alert the women at the next table as to its
presence? It would be a kindness, for mightn't they already be wondering why she had drawn her legs and feet
up onto the chair? It was only fair to allow them the same
posture. Not that a rat would *do* anything to their legs. It
was just that since time immemorial, women haven't
liked their legs to be in the vicinity of scuttling rats,
fearing that the rats will confuse them with ships' ropes
(hawsers), which rats are famous for traversing in the
expectation of their leading to the ship's larder.

However, she decided to say nothing to the women
about the rat. Ignorance is bliss; she pulled out one of the
all-time-great clichés, sister to What they don't know
can't hurt them, which she also summoned to reinforce
her desire to remain silent.

Lord knows they haven't been friendly to me. Nobody has. I'm a pariah. Everyone is afraid they'll catch my
face if they smile at me, and go away mutilated themselves.

Yesterday she had taken the stitches out by herself,

174

and she thought it was a great improvement. No one else seemed struck by this beautification project. Looking at her, they still flinched.

It is not easy, when you have been considered a beautiful woman all your life, to be made to feel monstrous. She did not know which was worse—to be stared at or to have the onlooker's eyes avert. She had different ideas of how to react to people's reactions, ranging from making a worse face by sticking out her tongue to looking noble and long-suffering. But she felt she must school herself from the beginning not to get caught up in the thing, to retain her inner self. She did not want to become angry or bitter, and she certainly did not want to become ennobled.

Anyhow, most of these tormentors were tourists. The Mexicans were nice. She thought that these Mayan-blooded Mexicans were particularly attractive, courteous, and kind.

She'd been six days at the Hotel Mayaland. After spending a few nights in Mérida, she'd hired a car and driver and taken the long, straight road through the three-tiered jungle to Uxmal, the way broken briefly by sisal plantations and small villages of round earthen homes with thatched roofs, peopled by spherical women, lean, honed men, nimble children.

It was hot but not horribly hot. It was the windy season, and the wind carried a suggestion of the sea, for the Gulf was not far away. She liked the hotel. Its cool tiled rooms and corridors opened to either balconies or flamboyant gardens. It was decorated with fine folk art, placed here and there by someone with amazing restraint.

Her physical weakness translated to a delicious lassitude, as she fell into the easygoing ways of the people.

Long, leisurely meals, followed by siestas. Each day she tried to do a little more. A swim. A walk. Each day she spent a couple of hours at Uxmal, strolling among the ruins, settling at one shady spot or another to gaze out over the mystifying ancient town, each separate perspective imbuing her with different thoughts and feelings. Who were the Maya? These people who, before Christ—yea, before the Egyptian civilization!—were so advanced in architecture, astronomy, math, and language? Were they survivors of the drowned Atlantis? The first wandering Jews? Mortals from a more sophisticated planet?

And why did they abandon these splendid cities? She felt empathy for the archaeologists and paleontologists, for she knew that deciphering the intricate stone carvings and the hieroglyphs must be akin to figuring out Mother Goose nursery rhymes.

But what she liked about it was the mystery. The unknowable was such a comfort, she thought, and ignorance among experts so delightful. It allowed for endless speculation.

Each day she climbed farther up the sheer stone pyramid of the Temple of the Magicians. The steps were steep and had not the depth to contain an entire forward foot so, she had to step sideways or use half a foot like climbing rungs rather than steps, and she had to come down as one would with a ladder, facing the stone. She still had about a hundred and fifty steep stone rungs to go before reaching the pinnacle. There was no hurry.

Just as she'd expected, she felt perfectly safe here in the jungle clearing. Her mind was resting and recovering, along with her body. She had stopped the head nodding, although there was backsliding.

But she didn't like seeing the rat. It struck her as a

portent, reminded her that she had let down her guard. But that's the whole idea! she exclaimed to herself. That's why I came here. So I could let down my guard and put all my energies into getting well. It's impossible to be on the qui vive and gain weight at the same time!

She put down her legs as if to show the rat and the world that she wasn't going to be dictated to by anyone or anything, least of all instinct.

The next day she doubled her previous distance up the pyramid, and at fifty feet was resting and catching her breath, when she saw a man descending agilely, facing outward, loose of limb, moving much in the way she had seen Joel blithely roam his building frames. He was a bleached-out figure against the dazzling blue sky, so it wasn't until he was ten feet away that she saw it was Dominic.

Oh, what a shock it gave her! Dominic here? Where she'd felt so safe at last? How? And, she added irrelevantly, whence? It was a lot like the mystery of the Maya, except there was no "who" about it, as this was definitely Dominic Racatelli, of Sicilian-Sicilian descent.

There was nothing at all she could do. It was too late to begin to pick her trembling way down. He had demonstrated his ease with the steep steps. So much so that he stopped to gloat, to look down on her, as it seemed to her, gloatingly.

"I've been waiting for you, Max, to get high enough. Do you understand?"

Yes, she understood. He would push her off the pyramid. It would be easy and efficient—very easy and efficient. And safe for him too. Everyone knew: the guides and tourists and concessionaires all knew how she came each day and tried to climb the pyramid, and how weak and pathetic she was at it. It would be no surprise to anyone that she had fallen.

She waited for her entire life to flash kaleidoscopically through her mind—as it is said to do at the point of death—curious to see the highlights. But, possibly because of her snake philosophy of shedding her past as she lived jubilantly on in the present, no pictures appeared. For a moment, confused, she wondered if she had lived at all. Maybe life indeed, as the poet said, or someone did, was all illusion.

Dominic, now, in the immediate present of the last moments of her life, was descending step by step toward her.

She thought how clever he had been to find her here, where he could perform the perfect murder.

She was glad she'd been right about him, glad she knew her man. All along she'd believed he'd come for her himself and kill her face to face, not send some hireling to shoot her in the back, boil her alive, or beleaguer her with roadkill.

She'd done well, though. She commended herself. Had she not eluded him for six long years?

She didn't mind dying too much. Except for Adam and the girls. It was intolerable to think she'd never see her babies again. Take care of each other, she whispered. Look after each other, okay? Tears rushed to her eyes, but she blinked them away. For Tom's sake, she'd die like a man.

She lifted her chin and looked straight and clear-eyed at Dominic. But he wasn't looking at her eyes; he was close enough now to see her livid skin graft. She saw a sort of shiver pass over his features—what the French would call a *frisson*. There was no English word quite like it, for it was a shiver that came from a ghastly thrill rather than from cold. How funny to have lexicological musings at the point of death.

"You're hurt," he said.

What a curious remark, she thought, as if it had just happened, as if I'd fallen down and scraped my knee. He is probably furious that someone got to hurt me before he did. This means he didn't light the fire. I knew he didn't. It's good to know you're right about things when you're going to be dead the next minute.

But Miliana was beginning to have an intuitive inkling that she wasn't going to die just yet.

He frowned and scrutinized her. "If I had not seen you first from afar, your walk, and if I had not known that you would be here at Uxmal, I would not know you now. You are completely altered. Yes, you look quite horrible." He smiled very slightly, a crooked, painful smile. "It is not just your face." He catalogued the rest. "You are old and gray and wasted."

This enraged Miliana. Fire leapt to her eye. I'll show him gray and wasted. He wants to see horrible? Her body bridled. But she had the good sense to realize that her appearance was causing a revulsion of feeling in him and that he was changing his plans accordingly. So, counter to all her best instincts, which were to show him she was every bit the woman she'd always been, she shrank away pitiably, letting her face and body go slack so that she looked, she hoped, older, if possible, and more wasted. Certainly she was bound to look quite witless.

"That's why you stood waiting for me so calmly," he said. "I would be doing you a favor to kill you now,

179

wouldn't I? Start down," he commanded her. "We will talk. Yes, I see I would have to talk to you in any case. I could not be satisfied with less."

She went ahead of him down the steps, then they walked abreast to the Governor's Palace, to sit in the shade of the wall. As they walked, Miliana took quick secret glances at Dominic. He was dressed in khaki pants and a blue polo shirt. He wore rope-soled shoes. His hair was rather long and still dark, although some bits of chest and back hair she could see were white. He looked fit, relaxed, and more affable, than she had ever known him to look. He, in his own way, had changed much more than she—for her change did not reflect her inner self and his, she believed, did.

They sat down on the stone and he talked. In the timeless silence of the ruins, his voice came with perfect fidelity. He told of his pursuit of her, which had become, in effect, a grand obsession. It had taken him all over the world. He had become not so much a pursuer as a seeker—such as those men who sought the Fountain of Youth, the Northwest Passage, Atlantis, or El Dorado. The Prester John of the Mafia was Dominic, the Peary of Malibu. It had changed his life. And him. Travel is so broadening, she mused, and seeking, it would seem, quite deepening. As well, it appears that he simply has not had the time to tend to his dastardly crimes. He is no longer the crooked man. He is a civilized human being.

And had not she changed too? she realized. Had not *being pursued* become something of a grand obsession of her own, heightening her daily experience to an incredible degree, along with her sensibilities and perceptions, and her appreciation for life. She remembered the luncheon with Soo Yung when it occurred to her to question whether portraying herself as perpetually endangered wasn't just a way to make her frivolous life appear profound. And she saw now that it had become profound, and as a result, she had a remarkable sense of herself. The fire, the burning, rather than deepening this sense, had almost eradicated it, made her weak and scared and dependent, made her the woman Dominic thought he saw before him, which was a false, fragile image she must at all cost sustain so as to trick him.

How he hated her! But it was such a healthy hate. It had not eaten him up; it had nourished him, caused him to flower.

"And now, at long last, I find you," he said. "If I had not known you were here, I would have passed you by like a stranger. What a joke that would have been after six years' searching. And yet it is true, Max. You are unrecognizable to me. What pleasure can I have in killing this old wreck who is not the woman I have pursued, not the Max who burned like a perpetual beacon, luring me on and on and on?"

Never mind the beacon business. It was the second time he had said he knew she was here. How did he know? Who told?

"You are such a pitiable creature," he went on. "Old, broken."

He makes me sound like a workhorse put out to pasture, she thought. A swayback. She started to sit up straight, then remembered the importance of the impression she was giving and again restrained her spirit, retained her broken hunch.

"You have no money and no friends."

He has not got his facts right, she thought. Boy, has he been misinformed. But I mustn't let him get a rise out of me.

"Your lovers are both unfaithful to you."

Well, that's true, she thought, but . . .

"And in any case would have nothing to do with you now." He gestured toward her mutilated face. Again the *frisson* passed across his features.

How can he sound so pleased by my disfigurement, Miliana wondered, when it obviously gives him such pain to look at me?

"Your daughters have put whole continents between you."

It only seems that way, she thought. A large distance between people does not signify a paltriness of love.

"And Adam will do the same."

Adam? That is his privilege. He must go where he will. You, poor Dominic, had always to abide by the will of your father. Adam can go anywhere, do anything.

"And your best friend sold you out, Max. Your best friend told me I would find you here in Uxmal—for a price."

Tom? Never. Certainly not Joel. And never in a million years Soo Yung.

For a price!

"What a sad story," said Dominic. "And how will it end? It won't. It will go on. I like it. I will like thinking of you like this. If ever I am feeling down, in years to come, I will think of you like this, Max: old and broken and ugly and friendless. It is much better than thinking of you dead. It will be like Wordsworth and his daffodils."

Ah, yes, she remembered. The poet saw a vast field of

daffodils one day that uplifted his spirit. Miliana's memory leapt to the poem's last lines, which Dominic was alluding to: "For oft, when on my couch I lie / In vacant or in pensive mood, / They flash upon that inward eye / Which is the bliss of solitude; / And then my heart with pleasure fills, / And dances with the daffodils."

It hadn't the pithiness of Mother Goose, but it was pretty good stuff.

But since when did Dominic read Wordsworth? Moreover, what on earth did he know about the bliss of solitude, he who would never let her leave his side for one second? She'd practically had to go to the bathroom with him.

Well, apparently his inward eye, which had previously turned upon putting her violently to death, was now to exult, to dance actually, with the vision of an old and swaybacked woman whose lovers after endless infidelities had left her flat, taking her children as models for successful and total departure, and whose best friend . . .

Who? she wondered. Which one? For a price!

But never mind; the main thing is that I'm alive. At least I think I am. I'm beginning to believe in this whole illusion business. After all, we're all molecules and have no substance. Even these old stones are a dream. And I am just to be, henceforth, a flash in Dominic's inward eye, and then only when he's down in the dumps.

Now Dominic was standing, about to leave. "What a woman you were once," he said wonderingly. "How are the mighty fallen!"

Another quote! She couldn't think who by. He'd certainly been doing a lot of reading. But not Mother Goose. If he had studied Mother Goose, as I have, Miliana thought contentedly, he would know that what he is looking at now is only how the illustrator has portrayed me.

Miliana had not spoken the whole time, but before Dominic left, she had to know. "Who?" she asked. "Which friend?"

"It would kill you to know. And you see, I don't want to kill you anymore. I will let you wonder. I will let it eat you up."

There was something else, which she wanted to know more. Would it give her away to ask? Would he scent the truth? That deep down she was wild and well and more of a woman than ever—that the present arrangement of her molecules was no more than a brilliant disguise.

She risked it. "Do you still play the piano?" she asked.

He shot her a searching look. He even reached out and whipped off her hat, as if she were hiding something from him. Quickly she covered her burn with her hand so the sun wouldn't touch it. Then she was afraid he'd see her real face, see that with the burn covered, that's all it was, a burn, a hurt, something foreign that had fallen on her face and would stay but not be integrated, something discrete and nonessential, trivial.

He didn't answer. "Do you?" he asked in return.

She did not reply, looked away.

He stood silently, waiting. Was he realizing he might have made a terrible mistake? What a fool she had been to speak. It touched on things too deep. Their life together. His giving her the gift of music, teaching her all he knew. The question was unbearably intimate. Also, if she did still play, it meant that she had something left, something maybe as good as, if not better than, money, lovers, health, youth. (Not children; nothing was better than children.)

Seeing that she would not speak, he threw her hat down at her feet, turned, and walked away.

Miliana replaced her hat and sat on. All around her the ancient stones told their secret stories. Unheard, like the music of the stars.

five

Meanwhile, back home, life went on.

Tom had begun an affair with the little blond muscular woman and was already tiring of her.

Joel was finishing the repairs to Miliana's house.

Predictably, Medical Bills, as Tom called her, still came around, perhaps taking advantage of Max's absence to establish herself in Joel's heart. She seemed to have learned a lot about Max. The one thing she didn't know— she never made reference to it—was that Max had been burned.

Joel knew that rivals were often intrigued about each other, but Medical Bills seemed more interested in Max than in him, the way she went on.

One day Joel was laying bricks for a fireplace he'd decided to put in Max's new bedroom, and Medical Bills had come by, bringing him a bag lunch. As usual, she talked of Max.

"I wonder if she'll keep coming to the beauty parlor when she gets back. Probably not, now that she knows I work there."

"She'd already stopped going, to save money," was Joel's answer to this.

"Well, you're going to see a big change in her looks!" she said with deep satisfaction.

"I'll see an even bigger change when I see her scars."

"Scars?"

"Yeah, from the burns. I only saw her with the bandages on."

Joel, who was carefully, even delicately, troweling putty onto a brick, didn't see her face change but heard it in her voice.

"I never knew that she got burned," she quavered. "Nobody told me. How could she have? She wasn't in the house when it was set fire to. That I know for certain."

"But when she saw it all in flames, she ran in to save Tom. She thought he was asleep. He—" Hearing footsteps, Joel turned and saw that she was leaving. He shrugged, thinking she'd be back. But she didn't come back . . . ever. He never saw Medical Bills again.

The Polynesian Investigator had gone on to other cases, leaving the Bartha house case, like most arson cases, unsolved.

Dub was still poking around. Miliana, had she known about Dub, would have guessed that because of the fire, Dominic suspected someone other than himself wanted Miliana dead and might still succeed in realizing that desire. Therefore the other must be discovered by him and not allowed to do her that "favor," as it could seriously jeopardize the satisfactory image he had constructed for his inward eye whenever he felt blue.

Fred had captured the "little blighter."

Soo Yung had cheered up and begun to spend the blood money. She moved to the Napa Valley, where she rented a cottage on a sunny spot of land, with a fruit tree in blossom right outside her door. She threw out all her old Chinese-style dresses, which years ago she'd had made for her in Hong Kong, and went to The Gap for jeans, to Saks for blouses and sweaters, and to Capellos for boots. She got a job that hadn't a thing to do with music: conducting tours through one of the larger California wineries.

So blood money wasn't so bad to have after all. Like any currency, it was a medium of exchange, and with it Soo Yung exchanged a rotten life for a nice one. It was the money that had the blood on it. What she bought with it was spotless.

Which leaves only one person unaccounted for, that being Miliana's neighbor the dog man.

He had the heavy-handed moniker of Caesar. People mostly called him Seez, except for some meanies who called him Sneeze. Seez was a clerk in a small hardware store downtown. He lived a minimal life in the house he had grown up in, first sharing it with both his parents, then with his mother, then his dog, and now he was alone, as one by one his family had been scythed away by the grim reaper. He had some friends among the minor merchants of the town but was essentially solitary.

When Joel came to work on Miliana's house, he treated the dog man with a jocular friendliness that was partly teasing and partly due to Joel's real goodheartedness. "Just the man I've been waiting for," he'd say heartily, as Seez came slinking out of his house, head ducked, shoulders hunched. "Join me in a beer, Seez old buddy. I know you're probably off on a hot date, but you have to share a cold one with me first. I'm counting on your companionship. A man gets weary of working alone all day.

And this is costing me enough, without putting someone else on the job."

Seez, amazed and blushing, would accept the proffered beer, hardly knowing what he was doing. Male camaraderie was something he'd never experienced.

In a couple of weeks, he adored Joel. Joel was his hero.

One Friday, Seez had made Joel a hot lunch and they were eating together out on Miliana's deck. Joel started talking about the fire. As he talked, he saw Seez grow increasingly uncomfortable, recrossing his legs a dozen times and busying himself with his napkin—wiping hands, mouth, and brow with it, and finally tying it in knots.

Joel continued: "That guy Bradley came by my place in the city one day and started asking me about your dog. I don't get that guy. What in heck would a dog have to do with a fire? He didn't know it was your dog Max was looking for. I told him it was. I suppose he came and talked to you about it."

"Uh, no. No, he didn't. What do you mean, *she* was looking for my dog?" he asked timidly, a little doglike yelp of surprise in his voice.

"I don't even know how he knew about the damn dog. I never knew a man to find out so much nonessential information. How many kids Max's ex-husband has, for God's sake." And Joel went on to tell Seez about the trailer incident. "Now, how did he know Max did that?"

"Well," Seez suggested tentatively, "don't you think he might have found out about it from the girl who was in the trailer?"

"But how would Bradley even begin to imagine anyone was inside the thing?" Joel said, yelping a little himself.

"Isn't that what investigators do? Uh . . . find out? Maybe she already knew Bradley."

"You might have something there, Seez. They're both English. In fact, they're both New Zealanders. Yeah, how about that?"

The light dawned. Joel even had some memory of seeing them together once. Yeah, he thought to himself, that night he took Max to dinner in Tiburon, she was sitting across the room with a blond guy. That's how Medical Bills knew so much about Max—from him, Bradley—and all the time I thought it was because of her knowing Max at the beauty shop.

"But about my dog . . ." Seez said.

"That damn dog. Miliana broke up with me on account of him." Joel shoved away his empty plate and got up to pace the deck.

"I'm sorry, Joel." Seez *was* sorry. He couldn't stand to be in any way, even indirectly, a cause of Joel's unhappiness. But he didn't understand and he wanted to, so he persevered. "I've lost my dog, you know," he said, trying to start at the beginning, hoping to learn something.

Now it was Joel who looked uncomfortable. Lacking a napkin to fiddle with, he raked his hands through his hair. "Yeah, well, you see, Seez, I got pissed off at the mutt for getting on my car, so I hauled it over to the East Bay and left it there. Max was real upset and dumped me because of it. Up until the time of the fire, she was looking for it so she could give it back to you. That's what Tom told me anyhow." Joel threw himself back down in the deck chair. "The snoop actually found the dogcatcher who she'd paid to make an extra effort to find him. He hasn't caught him yet, but he's seen him."

Seez moaned. "Oh, Lordy. I thought *she'd* taken him. I blamed her. I was so mad. I've been feeling all the time like the fire was my fault because I really wanted something awful to happen to her. I wanted her to get hurt for taking my dog. I used to follow her all around, wishing a calamity on her but not getting up nerve to do anything myself. Sometimes I do believe I was in such a state that I might have set that fire myself and then forgot I did it. I've had fits like that before. I get depressed and do bad things. Oh, Joel!" He fell to his knees and put his head in his arms on Joel's lap.

Joel had never felt so embarrassed in his life. He turned beet red, a blush Seez himself might have aspired to. But since nobody was around to see them, Joel just said, comfortingly, "There, there," and patted Caesar's head.

Tom arrived and walked through the house to the deck. When he saw Seez with his head on Joel's lap, he rolled his eyes and said, "Oh, man!" and looked even more embarrassed than Joel.

"Seez, here, thinks he set the fire," Joel explained, giving Seez a nudge so he'd get up on his feet, which he sheepishly did. "Seez, this is Tom Flynn."

"If he thinks he set the fire," said Tom, "why don't you kick his teeth in instead of saying 'There, there'?"

"I don't think he did it. He just thinks he might have, because he was so upset about his dog disappearing."

"Let's go over the day of the fire," Tom said, sitting down and grabbing a beer from Joel's cooler. "Seez, try to remember. Did you see anything or anyone out of the ordinary that day?"

Seez, flustered, talked fast. "I . . . I saw you, I saw the

blond man and the neighbor who sent in the alarm and the firefighters and the ambulance men." He sounded so excited it was as if he was reliving the experience.

"The blond man?" Joel said. "That was Bradley, the insurance investigator, right?"

"I don't know," said Seez, looking ashamed, wanting to please and to help.

"You mean you've never talked to Bradley?"

Seez shook his head woefully.

"That's funny. He's talked to everyone else, and you should have been the first—an actual witness."

"It's damned queer," said Joel. "Bradley goes all the way to the East Bay to talk to a dogcatcher but doesn't talk with Max's neighbor, who was here when the fire was set? And even when he finds out the dog belonged to the same neighbor, he still doesn't talk to him? The man's a jerk."

Tom had been staring at Seez. Now he said, angrily, "This is the man who followed Miliana when she left the hospital, the one I thought was familiar."

"Yeah, he was just telling me he followed her around."

"I kept hanging around the hospital for a glimpse of her," Seez explained to Tom. His eyes grew wide, remembering. "She looked hideous. I was glad, too. Now I learn that she didn't take my dog from me; Joel did. And she broke up with Joel because of it."

Tom looked at Joel, surprised—and hurt. Yet another thing Max had not revealed to him.

"Oh, I hope I didn't do it," Seez wailed. He stuffed the now thoroughly knotted napkin in his mouth as if to gag himself.

"Well, think the hell back, will you?" Tom said, exas-

192

perated. "Did you see me leave on my hike that morning? What did you do then?" When Seez just said, "Mmmph," Tom said grimly, "Take the fucking napkin out of your mouth."

"I can't remember. I can't."

"Did you see Miliana drive off in my car?" Tom persisted.

"I might have," he said hopefully. "If I did, I wouldn't have set the fire, would I, because she wouldn't be there to get hurt."

"Did you ever mess with her hot tub?"

Seez wrung his hands. "I think I did. I might have. I don't know what I was thinking about. Oh, Lord, help me and save me. Lord beat me to blisters."

"Oh, shut up about the Lord. You're in big trouble. And if you ask me, you're a looney tunes."

"Take it easy," Joel said to Tom. "Let the guy be. You can see he's all upset and doesn't know what he's saying."

"I should turn myself in. I should go to this investigator and tell him everything." He got up and started backing away from them both. "That's what I'll do," he said. "I'll make a clean breast." He stopped backing, then came forward and gathered the plates. "Bradley, is it? I'll go see him right now, I promise."

"Miwok Insurance Company," Tom said. "Get going."

"Thanks for the lunch," Joel said pityingly.

Tom and Joel were quiet, sipping their beers. After a bit, Tom said, "I didn't know Max dumped you."

"Now you know," said Joel. Then he asked, "Did she look that awful?" He'd been dwelling on what Seez had said about seeing her when she left the hospital.

"Yeah, she did."

"Hideous? Would you say hideous?"

"No," Tom said sadly. "I wouldn't say hideous."

"Tom, what're you going to do?"

"Stay with her. Be her man. But I didn't know it was over between you. That makes it harder."

"Miliana won't want pity, you know."

"What am I supposed to do? No man's going to look at her now. Anyhow, I love her. I just wish I was a better person. I just don't know if I can stay true to her. Or to anyone, really. But now, if I am unfaithful, it will seem cruel. Then I'll start to resent her. It's going to be tough."

"Do you want to put your head in my lap and cry?" Joel said scornfully.

"It's easy for you," Tom said, feeling depressed—feeling more depressed, rather, since he already was in a pretty bad way. "It's over between you. You build her a new bedroom and you're square."

"I built it for love. I love Miliana. I've never spent a boring minute with that woman. But she wouldn't have me in the long run. She probably won't have you either. She's got other fish to fry."

Tom looked surprised. "What do you mean?"

"If you ask me, she still loves her husband."

"Dominic? You're kidding."

"I could be wrong, but it seems like all this being chased to the death by him, right or wrong, allowed her to keep thinking about him the whole time. Every day! It kept him the most important one."

"Then why did she leave him?" Tom asked.

"Because he was a crook and she's honest as the day is long. And because she couldn't stand losing her identity, which was what was happening. She's a strong woman, but he was stronger."

"Still, there's no way she'll go back to him. And that leaves me. She's going to be very dependent."

"Not Max."

"You haven't seen her with the bandages off. She'll never be the same. Or, worse, she'll be a mockery of herself."

"It's just a piece of her face," Joel said angrily, as angry as Tom had been with Seez. "We're just talking about a piece of skin here, for Christ's sweet sake."

"You're free," Tom said again. "It's easy for you to say."

"Then maybe now's my time to get her back from you," Joel said with a glint to his eye. "Because now's the time when she needs a real man."

Joel went back to his sheetrocking. Tom sat on, looking out at the view, having another beer, thinking about manliness.

Seez quickly washed his dishes, dried them, and put them away. He then put on a black polyester suit and a tie, got into his Toyota, and drove to the city, to Miwok Insurance.

Joel, the greatest man who ever lived, believed in him, and he hoped to prove that he was worthy of Joel's trust. He knew he had done some bad things. He had a dream-like memory of monkeying with Miliana's hot tub, and he clearly remembered putting a vermin carcass on her stoop, but he just didn't think he had set fire to her house. He hoped very much that Mr. Bradley could assure him he hadn't.

Seez slunk into the intimidating-looking insurance company offices. Bradley wasn't in, but his secretary said he'd be back by the end of the day, so Seez waited, sweating in his dark suit. It was shortly before five when Bradley appeared. Seez was let into his office to see him and found there was nothing to say.

"Yes?" said Bradley, brusquely. "What is it? Can I help you? Well?"

Seez just stared.

"My secretary says you are here in connection with the Bartha case. Do you have some information for me? The case is closed, to all intents and purposes."

Seez looked at the ground.

"I gather you are Ms. Bartha's neighbor, Mr. Caesar Smith. The information I have about you is that you are an antisocial person and often a town nuisance, a borderline personality. It occurred to me that, upset as you were at losing your pet, you might have been making more than a nuisance of yourself to Ms. Bartha. You have a record of behaving maliciously because of imagined slights. However, I decided not to proceed along those lines and instead closed the case on her fire."

Seez gasped something out.

"I beg your pardon? I didn't hear you. Just as well. You'd do well to keep your mouth shut. That will be all, Mr. Smith."

Bradley got up from behind his desk and opened the door for Seez. He put out his hand and Seez spit on it profusely, proving Bradley's information regarding Seez's nuisance value to be quite correct.

Seez then gave a bobbing little bow to the astonished secretary. Ducking his head, hunching his shoulders, he cringed his way out.

six

*F*or a month, *Miliana dedicated herself* to her renewal. She felt that Dominic, unwittingly though it may have been, had thrown down the gauntlet. He had seen her as weak, old, afraid, broken, and mutilated, and he had not been that far wrong, because what she'd been doing in the Yucatán was hiding, licking her wounds, feeling sorry for herself, pretending to recover from her accident but in fact nurturing her weakness.

Now she embarked on a serious course of nourishment, rest, and exercise. As well, she took an interest in her looks. She kept her face, neck, and shoulders from the sun but let the rest of her body lightly tan. The sun bleached her hair as the bottle had used to do. It had been thick and wavy, worn brushed high off her forehead, but now it had thinned, along with her body, and grown long. She trained it to fall in deep waves around her face, so that the wound was mostly obscured. She forswore her shirts and pants and wore the native dress of the Yucatán: white colorfully embroidered shifts over the longer white-eyelet petticoats, with the difference that she sashed in the waist, since, unlike Mayan women, she had a waist. She journeyed to other ruins—Tulum, Chichén Itzá, Palenque—but Uxmal remained her favorite.

The Temple of the Magicians, which was to have been instrumental in her death, seemed more than any other place to instill in her the force of life—perhaps, too, the force of Dominic. His presence was there now, deep in the stones with the Maya. Maybe, in a way, she kept returning there daily to be with him, because Dominic, or the idea of Dominic, had been such an important part of her everyday existence that she seemed unable to relinquish it entirely, or to believe that it no longer had any thrust.

This is not so surprising, she comforted herself. It is like anything else that you have lived with intimately for a long time—a disease, a million dollars, a child, beauty. When one day you are formally informed that you no longer have that thing or person, it would take some time to *feel* that you were without it, to act as if you no longer had it, and even if it had been a bad thing, you would miss it extremely, so much a part of you had it become.

So much a part that it *was* you. I am my flight from Dominic.

But if so, it would mean that my leaving Dominic six years ago, to separate myself from the inseparable, didn't really work at all. He was as much a part of me during these years when I believed myself to be independent as when we were wholly together—only in a different guise.

She found herself unable to climb the pyramid but figured that was natural under the circumstances. She would stand at the foot of it, hesitating. It was too late in the day or too early, too windy or too hot. Then she would admit to herself, "I haven't the strength," and promise to try another day.

Whenever she found herself brooding about the friend who had sold her out, she stopped, determined not to let it "eat her up." It was too awful to contemplate. Tom? Joel? Soo Yung? No! Unthinkable! She would deal with it when she got home. How, she was not sure. She had pulled a fast one on Dominic, a brilliant maneuver, but he had planted this destructive seed, which must not be allowed to flourish or she would become the paltry woman he believed her to be. At the same time, she knew she must address it eventually. Denial makes a good fertilizer too, the only difference being that the malignancy grows unbeknownst to the body that houses it. Yes, she would address it, but first she would grow strong.

She wondered where Dominic had gone and how often old swayback flashed upon his inward eye. She wondered if there was a hole in his life too, without his grand obsession to absorb his every waking minute, a hole in his self. Did he feel this same weird, cavernous emptiness that she did?

On the plane home, Miliana took pen in hand for the first time since leaving the hospital, to try to illuminate what she had come to call the Judas quandary. She titled the essay "Blood Money in Mother Goose." Though she didn't have success finding any there, it made her feel good to write about Jesus.

Everyone knows the Judas story. Judas took money and sold out his best friend, who subsequently was crucified on a cross.

Judas Iscariot was one of Jesus Christ's disciples. He accepted thirty pieces of silver to point Jesus out to his enemies. Only it was worse than pointing. He said, "Whomsoever I shall kiss, that same is he; take him."

Is that low? Name me, if you can, something more foul than putting a finger on a man with your lips, turning the tenderest caress into a death notice.

Jesus knew. Turning his lambent gaze on Judas, he said, "Betrayest thou the son of man with a kiss?" Oh, how those words must have reverberated in the heart of

Judas! How long could you live with that? Two days, tops.

When Jesus was condemned, two days later, Judas cast the thirty pieces of silver down before the priests who had paid him, declared that he had sinned, then went and hanged himself.

The priests did not put the money in the treasury, because *it was the price of blood.*

Jesus had known what was in the cards for him, and shortly before all this came to pass, he said to his gathered disciples: "Verily, verily I say unto you that one of you shall betray me"—whereas I never dreamed that one of my (I can hardly call them disciples, although the idea is pleasing) friends would betray me to Dominic.

Would that I could go to each one of them and say that beautiful sentence, "Betrayest thou me with a kiss?"

Then whichsoever one went straightaway and hanged himself, he would be the Judas. Maybe he *has* hanged himself. Maybe I'll arrive home to find that one of my friends is dead. The thought does not give me any pleasure.

The trouble is—and this is actually a big trouble—I'm not dead. Therefore my Judas has got off scot-free, has tucked away a tidy sum and is none the worse for it.

Mother Goose says, "For every evil under the sun / There's a remedy, or there is none. / If there be one, try to find it; / If there be none, never mind it."

If only I could never mind it. I want to arrive home and fall into the arms of my dear ones. The very nature of returning home is going lickety-split to see your friends so as to get reestablished in their hearts and they in yours, and sharing all your recent adventures, although it's true that friends *never* want to hear about your travels—they're much more interested in telling you about their latest trip to the market.

But we're talking betrayal here.

Oh, if only it hadn't happened. If only I didn't have to deal with it. Tom wouldn't betray me. He saved my life. Unless for some reason he couldn't bear the burden of that responsibility, felt that by so saving me, he was bound to look after me forevermore, and he'd see me dead first.

Joel? Are you kidding? Joel has so much money he wouldn't do it for gain. And if he were really angry with me, he'd confront me on the spot, not tell Dominic my whereabouts, then go and rebuild my house. Of course, it *would* be a way of getting paid for the building job.

And Soo Yung? Why? There is simply no reason in the world for her to do such a terrible thing.

You may have guessed by now that there is no blood money in Mother Goose or in any poems or stories I can think of except the Bible. So Jesus is my only guideline, but he's too good for me to emulate. So resigned was he, so forgiving, so meek.

He knew Judas would betray him but was surprised and hurt by the method. Therefore that sad, yet essentially mild, reproach, ". . . with a kiss?"

No, meek I am not. Nor do I feel angry, vengeful, or hurt. What I feel is embarrassed. I'm embarrassed not to be dead. And I'm embarrassed for whichsoever friend it was that he fell so low. I quite quail at the idea of exposing him, because we will *both* feel so mortified. But expose him I must.

Being betrayed is the one thing you can't go around pretending didn't happen.

Here is a rhyme by old Mother Maximiliana:

There was an old woman lived under a hill,
Pursued by a crooked sir.
When finally he found her, he looked all around her
And said, You are not what you were.

He whipped off her hat and said, That is that,
Your Judas won't hang by a noose.
Your Judas won't care that I gave you a scare,
There's no blood money in Mother Goose.

Adam met her at the airport. They exchanged a spon-
taneous glad embrace that got the other arrivals all grin-
ning at the happiness of it. Miliana's eyes drank in her
son, for she remembered vividly the moment she'd whispered her goodbye on the pyramid and how wrung her
heart had been at the thought of never seeing her children
again.

"You look so pretty!" he said.

Already she felt silly in her Mexican clothes, which is
always the way with ethnic garb once one is away from
its country of origin, but no matter. Adam found her
pretty.

"I'm a new woman," she told him while driving home,
feeling, after her month in the green still jungle primeval,
a little stunned at the magnitude of the silver city, its
hustle and bustle, financial towers reaching for the sky,
bridges stretching across water for something stable to
land on. "Dominic and I have had our *dénouement* and I am
no longer as one pursued. I can live a normal life, get a job,
a driver's license, and never again need I look behind me
to see if someone's following."

Adam looked at her curiously. Her voice, he thought,

had a conscious lilt to it, as if covering up a disappoint-ment.

"It will take some getting used to," she added. Then, after a moment, she said, "Tell me the news."

"But I don't understand about Dominic," said Adam. "Wasn't he out to get you after all?"

Miliana would have liked to tell Adam the story. She felt proud of her coup. But he might not see it that way, might not feel it was to her credit that his mother, Miliana the fearless, got out of a tight spot by pretending to be old and retarded.

It was only natural that he would hope to hear some stirring account of their meeting on the pyramid, a Joan-of-Arcian triumph of good over evil culminating in a James Bondian chase scene up and down the pyramids, over the roof of the Governor's Palace at night, with the light and sound show they put on for tourists *(luz y sonido)* highlighting them in pink and green and blue, while the cornball legends of the Maya rolled sonorously over the staccato shots of guns.

She felt sure Adam would not relish the true vision of his mother picking her trembling way down the pyramid, slack-jawed, thin, and bent, with long, knuckly hands. And he would not like to know that Dominic had seen her like that—worse than if he'd caught her scrubbing floors. Come to think of it, *she* didn't like Dominic seeing her that way either, but it had saved her life, so who was she to carp?

Nevertheless, one had to maintain one's image with one's son. "I outfoxed him, sweetheart. I was so clever that he doesn't even know that I pulled a gigantic fast one on him. Someday I will tell you the story but not now."

"What about the money?"

"The money? There was no mention made of it. The money, you see, was never an issue. I wonder why nobody can understand that. Everyone seems to have a chronic case of money on the brain, like water on the knee. The truth of the matter is that Dominic is one of the few people, maybe the *only* one, I've known who doesn't give a hoot about money."

"What if he finds out you pulled this gigantic fast one?"

"He won't. He'll forget about me now and get on with his life. Which is just what I'm going to do."

Again Adam detected a forlorn note. But all in all, he felt happy about how his mother looked and seemed. The Temple of the Magicians had done the trick, given her the answer, whatever it was—whatever the question was.

They were crossing the Golden Gate Bridge now. On the bay below, which was often in the throes of a nautical festival of one kind or another, a multitude of windsurfers were strung across the water like migrating butterflies. A fireboat, releasing its graceful arcs of water, was greeting an arrival in the bay, which she now saw nosing its way under the bridge, an aircraft carrier, looking bigger than Alcatraz Island. Phalanxes of sailors stood at attention on the deck. All very stirring, but she didn't like to contemplate how the butterflies would give way to it.

"Before I tell you the news," said Adam, "I have to tell you that Dr. Miyami freaked out when he heard you'd left the hospital without his say-so. You were supposed to have some special treatments. I promised him you'd come to see him as soon as you got back."

"Okay. But tell me, is the house finished?"

"Joel has built you a sensational bedroom, much bigger, and with a fireplace in it."

"Really?"

"The dogcatcher has found the neighbor's dog."

"Good."

"I ran a four forty-nine fifteen hundred."

"A P.R.! I'm so proud of you, sweetheart. That's fast!"

"And," he said, "an even bigger breakthrough, I've fallen for a girl who isn't pretty."

"That is impressive. But do you go about openly with her or take side roads?"

"I take side roads, but still . . ."

Still and all.

Miliana sneaked an anxious look back to the bay before they entered the Waldo Tunnel. Joy being more flexible than might, the windsurfers were still weaving their myriad ways over the water, while the carrier, stony-faced, had come to a stop.

Adam told her more about his new girlfriend, who was a long jumper and almost as big and strong as he was, which, distance runners being slight, was not alarming. Then he got back to news of Miliana's friends.

"Soo Yung has moved to the Napa Valley, and she wants you to visit when you can."

"Imagine!"

"Bradley didn't find the arsonist and has closed the case.

"Joel says your neighbor, the dog man, whose name is Caesar, might have torched your house because he thought you'd killed his dog. But Joel wants to clear Seez, and he's gotten suspicious of some girlfriend of his who he hasn't heard from since she found out about your burns. He discovered she left town. Pretty fishy, he says. Apparently, just an hour or so before the fire, you pushed over a trailer that she was in, so it could have been her way of getting revenge. I didn't hear about *that* one. You never rest, do you?"

"I didn't know she was in the trailer, poor thing. She probably heard I was returning from the jungle and left town for fear I'd inflict further violence on her. I'm sure she didn't set the fire. She looked like the sort who wouldn't hurt a fly." She laughed. "I told her never to fool around with Maximiliana Bartha and she shivered in her shoes.

"But my goodness, Adam, this is a lot of news; almost too much to integrate. How is Tom? You haven't even mentioned Tom."

"He seems a bit depressed, if you ask me. He's on duty right now and tried to do a trade so he could be with you this evening, but no luck. Call him when you get home."

So none of her friends had hanged themselves, but Tom was depressed.

"I'm sorry to hear he's feeling down." Miliana was thoughtful. "Adam, do me a favor; I don't want you to tell anyone that I saw Dominic. Not a soul, okay?"

"Sure. No problem. Any more work on your legacy?"

"Not very much. Just one rather slight piece. But don't worry, I'll go on with it. I'm not feeling so pressed to get it finished, now that I'm not going to die."

seven

*M*iliana *anxiously scanned Tom's face* for any signs of epic betrayal. It was Sunday afternoon, the day after her return. They were uneasy with each other. She had been unable to throw herself wholeheartedly into his welcoming embrace. How could she, until she knew for sure whether or not he was the Judas?

"I don't want to rush back into our relationship," she said, almost at once. "We must see where we are with each other, feel our way carefully back toward each other. I am different."

And she remembered Byron again: "I am not now that which I have been." But she knew that quote no longer obtained, as it implied a failing, a being less. I am not less, she realized. I am only different. Perhaps I am more. "How are the mighty fallen!" Dominic had said. Well, the mighty are picking herself up again.

"You look wonderful, Max," Tom said, thinking she needed reassurance. "Really, you do. I'm amazed!"

He was sincere. She did look good. Although she did not burn with her bright flame of old, he thought she had a lovely light about her, a magical glow. Her blond lashes, no longer tinted, made her eyes seem even darker, a dark golden brown. Already he felt so much better. Just to be with her! And to think he'd been dreading her return, fearing what he conceived to be the burden of her love, and of his responsibility to her.

Of course, she probably knew exactly what he was feeling and now was trying to set his mind at ease by withdrawing from him. That's the kind of woman she was. How could he have imagined differently? It was just that he'd been feeling so low. And, he realized now, the reason he had was that he had missed her so much. He'd been marking time until her return, when he could begin to live again. He remembered Joel saying he'd never spent a boring minute with her. What if Joel did try to get her back? Would she go? What did he mean, she had other fish to fry?

Tom had walked into her house wondering how to get rid of her and now, within minutes, felt frightened of losing her.

"Max!" He reached out for her again, but she whisked by him to the kitchen, saying, "I got us a piece of fish and a lovely white zinfandel. But first we have to go and see the dog man. I have a surprise for him."

Tom is in a state, she thought. He seems to be feeling guilty about something for sure. I don't like this at all. It certainly is no fun being betrayed by a best friend. I don't think it's much fun being the betrayer either. I know that Judas didn't think so for very long. But I will just die if it's Tom.

"I'm sorry," he said.

Sorry? She reflected on the inadequacy of the word if it was to usher in the confession of his betrayal. Sorry? Wouldn't the word "suicidal" be more apropos? And rending his clothes while speaking would be a nice touch.

Even while she made these jokes to herself, her heart sank that it might be so. No, Tom, she cried inwardly. Not you. Don't let it be you. She looked out the window with a passionate desire to see a cow jumping over the moon. She could not bear life being so serious. So real.

Saved! There was a knock at the door and Tom let in the neighbor man. Seez held a big bouquet of flowers. "Welcome home," he said miserably. "I'm sorry."

Another supplicant, she thought, or perhaps penitent is more the word. Everyone's apologizing. How intolerable to come home to all these wretched faces. "Have I got a big surprise for you!" she said jollily, taking the flowers but ignoring his words. "Stay there."

She went to her bedroom and returned with his damnable dog. "I went over and got him today and was just waiting for you to get home." She unclipped the leash and the little dog ran to Seez, jumping into his outstretched arms.

The pooch went into an ecstatic fit. He whined and barked and yelped, all at the same time. He wiggled and wagged and licked. Seez burst into tears.

Tom rolled his eyes and said, "Oh, man," and Miliana stood with her hands clasped together, beaming on the two of them, man and dog.

"I've got to talk to you," Seez blubbered.

"I know, but now's not a good time. I've hardly said hello to Tom. As you hardly have to your dog. Let us now separately expand on our greetings to our loved ones. Later we can talk together."

The dog had now subsided into silence, with his paws on Seez's shoulders, his head on his chest. Seez clasped him to his bosom. He himself, however, had not subsided, and was still weeping abundantly. It wasn't clear whether they were tears of happiness re dog or guilt re Miliana, for he kept trying to get on with his apology even while lavishing his dog with hugs and pats. "I went to see Bradley to tell him I might have set the fire—"

"Off you go now," Miliana said, feeling that she was almost begging him to go at this point and that they should be quits with each other now that she had returned his dog. She did not want to become friends and neighbors. She would never borrow sugar from him. She didn't want to discuss the fire. She didn't even care. The Judas quandary had thrown the fire in the shade. The fire was past history. In her philosophy of life as a snake, it was simply another skin to be shed—although granted that bit of personal history had taken more than its fair share of skin.

"I think you should go straight home and feed your little mutt. I don't keep any dog kibble around because Tom scorns it."

Seez resisted, was determined to speak. "He was the blond man I saw on the day of the fire."

"Tom." She turned away from Seez to beseech Tom. "I just don't want to talk about the fire. Will you get him to go?"

"Hang it up, Seez." Tom pushed him toward the door. The dog started to growl warningly, but Tom ignored him. "We've already been through this," Tom said. "We don't want to hear any more about it." He put him through the door and closed it just as the dog snapped at his arm and narrowly missed.

"But it was *before* the fire," Seez called through the door.

Tom stood there. "What was?" he asked Miliana. "What was before the fire?"

But Miliana said sorrowfully, "Why couldn't you have greeted me like that little dog did him, thrown yourself on my bosom, barking ecstatically?"

"You were the cold one."

"You were cold first."

"That's what I started to apologize about. I was feeling scared—that you'd want too much of me now, more than I can give. But now I realize I *can* give that much, and you'd never ask it of me anyhow."

Miliana smiled sadly. "That statement doesn't make any sense. But," she said, holding up her hand, "don't try to say it again. I really don't want apologies from you or Seez or anyone. I didn't even care so much about your chilling greeting until I saw that dumb dog greet Seez, and then I felt jealous. Then I thought, Shouldn't I be able to expect at least half that much joy from my lover I haven't seen for over a month? Instead he greets me with such a long face his chin is dragging on the ground. It makes me think you didn't want me to come back." She paused and said meaningfully, "That maybe you didn't *expect* me to come back."

She searched his face, looked at him keenly, but he didn't blanch or quiver. His face just kept looking long and absolutely adorable. Maybe he hadn't heard her. She remembered that he was deaf.

"You didn't even kiss me on the mouth," he groused, "just gave me a peck on the cheek. What the hell, I thought. What's going on here?"

"I couldn't let you kiss me because of Judas."

Now they were getting down to it. Again she put the spotlight of her keen glance on him, but nothing was revealed, nothing.

"Judas who?"

"Iscariot," she said dryly.

"I don't know him. Is he a fireman? There's a guy with a name like that at station fourteen."

"He betrayed Jesus with a kiss."

211

"You mean all this is because I slept with some dumb blonde while you were away? That was another thing I was afraid of—that you'd start to get all upset by every little infidelity and lay guilt trips on me."

"I've never laid a guilt trip in my life," she said hotly.

"Well, what's this?"

"We're not talking some minor infidelity here, we're talking massive betrayal. *Blood money.*" This was it now. She couldn't lay it on the line any more forcefully without outright asking him if he'd sold her out to Dominic.

"Oh, so that's it. You've got your menstrual period. I should have known. You're always cranky and unreasonable when you're on the rag. Let's open the wine, shall we?"

Miliana felt a huge flood of relief, certain now that Tom was not the one. "Yes, let's," she said.

"Then let's go christen your new bedroom. I'm not a man to let a little blood stop me. Especially if you're going to pay me. We're setting a precedent here, you understand. Every time we make love during your menses, I get money. It's called blood money."

"Fair enough." Miliana laughed heartily. It was the first time she'd laughed since she'd left the hospital and Tom made the joke about her trench coat. Did it feel good!

After their lovemaking, they lay on the bed, sipping the mauve-colored wine. "Your body's different," Tom said.

"It's the swimming, maybe. Developed my upper body a bit."

"You're still thin."

"I know. I eat, but I don't seem to gain. I still don't feel very strong. I wish I did. I guess it takes longer to recover when you're older. I feel so happy right now. That was a nice greeting, Tom. Thank you."

It *was* a nice greeting. But her body had been curiously unresponsive. It wasn't just the orgasm, or lack of it, for she could have one or not and it was not a big issue with her. She did not make a cult of coitus and loved the whole act for its infinite variety of feelings and sensations (especially orgasm). Still, her body had felt (she hated to say it) dead. She hoped it hadn't felt that way to Tom. She hoped she'd made up for it with all that her heart felt, her true happiness at being in his arms once again, wholly connected. There could be lots of reasons for her physical absence, but she was going to be damned if she'd analyze it now. Or ever.

"Now I really feel I'm home. And isn't the bedroom beautiful! Look at those redwood beams. And that fireplace tucked into the corner, nice as you please."

"Joel did a great job, all right. Tell me about your trip."

"I will, but first I want to say don't worry. I'm not going to ask anything of you. I'm going to be moving along in a little while." She noticed he wasn't listening. Maybe he hadn't heard. "Tom, what are you thinking?"

"He said, 'before the fire.' "

"Seez?"

"He saw Bradley here before the fire. Man, this is getting weird. But Seez could be confused. He's got trouble in the attic, that guy. He's only rowing with one oar. Still, I knew a guy once, used to go around at night breaking store windows. He was a glazier, needed the business."

"Meaning Bradley sets fires so he can investigate them? What an extraordinary idea."

"No. So he could investigate *you.* And it would explain why Bradley never interviewed Seez, realizing Seez might have seen him that morning when he was committing the crime.

"Also, it would explain why he was so scared when Joel and I came bursting into his office." Tom told her about that day, and Miliana's bosom swelled with pride in her two knights-errant.

"My heroes," she said. "I hope this turns out to be the answer. It's a comfort to know that no one was really trying to do me an injury. I'm safe from everyone now, Tom, even Dominic. Listen. . . ."

Miliana told Tom the story of meeting Dominic on the pyramid, exactly as it happened, making it sound scary and exciting. He was enthralled. She did not include the announcement that one of her three best friends had sold her out. She was confident now that it wasn't Tom (oh, joy!), and why let him think that it had entered her mind for a minute that it might be he. It would break his heart. It had almost broken hers.

"What's this about moving on, then, if you're not pursued anymore? You're not really going to be leaving, are you, Max?"

"Yes, sweetheart, I am."

"Are you afraid that Dominic might get a glimpse of you now, looking so lovely, and find out it wasn't true"—he paused to kiss her scar—"that it was all a big act?"

"No. He likes thinking of me as the woman who, because she left him, lost everything: her beauty, youth, health, and the love of her lovers and children. As far as he's concerned, it's all over. The big pursuit is ended and he likes the ending. He wouldn't change it for the world. He won't be looking for me anymore."

eight

How wrong Miliana was. About everything!

Dominic lay on his bed in the bedroom of his suite at the Huntington Hotel, where he was able to get superior rooms without a view, hard to find in San Francisco. Dominic didn't like views. He smoked a cigar and watched the smoke hang over his head. He appreciated the way cigar smoke briefly patterned the air rather than fusing with it at once.

This was the sort of thing Dominic had been doing for the last month, ever since his *"dénouement"* with Miliana on the pyramid—lying on hotel beds, watching smoke, seeing pictures in the patterns. Those were the exciting days. On other days, he lay on the bed not smoking.

He'd only been on this particular hotel bed for a few days. At the moment, he was waiting for Dub to return from an errand and he was, not for the first time, reviewing his meeting with Max.

He had gone to Uxmal to kill her.

He waited for her on the pyramid. When he saw her and said, "I've been waiting for you to get high enough. Do you understand?" he was still going to kill her. He was going to push her off.

Over the years, Max had become an idea, a fixed idea. It is easy to hate an idea, not so easy to hate a person, impossible to purely hate someone you hopelessly love.

As he descended the pyramid toward her, she became

first a flesh-and-blood human, as opposed to an idea, and then the one person in all the world that was Max, she whom he had met and instantly loved, who had marked his heart forever. He was as overwhelmed at that moment as he had been at their original meeting. All his feelings of love and yearning came flooding back to him on a tidal wave of emotion that was increased tenfold by her vulnerability and by the way she stood waiting for him so clear-eyed and unafraid.

Confused, unmanned, powerless, he attacked her verbally instead of physically, and saw at once that he had his out. He would not have to kill her if he could pretend pleasure and satisfaction in letting her live. And he saw how, believing him, she played along, saw how she tried to make herself appear to be all that he pretended.

When he was close enough to see her scars, he almost could not go on with the pretense. He only wanted to take her in his arms and cover her with kisses, bathe her wounds with his tears. All the hatred he'd felt at the idea of Max was now transferred to the person who had hurt her.

Meanwhile he kept up his act. Excoriatingly he slashed away at her with his tongue. He saw her spirit straining to break loose and engage with him, saw her rein it in with all her might, bite her own tongue to quell its expression.

How very much he admired her. How touched he was by her whole being. How grateful he was to her, for it was because of Max, his love for her, and his hate, that he had been transformed, that he had lived.

Before he left her, he removed her hat so he could take in every lineament of her beautiful, beautiful face. If she'd looked at him then, she'd have seen all, known all, but she resolutely looked away.

Now they were both successfully free of this pursuit and flight that had chained them, and, luckily, they each had something to do: Max to find her betrayer, he to find the fire-starter. These activities would bridge the awful gulf their make-believe resolution had created.

Then what?

He knew that Max had dealt with his hate better than with his love. His love had been too much for her. Would she consider trying again with him? If she did, would he be able to love her in the halfhearted way she required, in the way that Joel and Tom loved her?

No. Never! Impossible!

He stirred restlessly on the bed and mashed out his cigar.

When he heard a knock on his door he didn't bother to rise. "Come in."

Dub entered, radiating cheer. "I got the information, boss," he said happily, tossing down an enormous packet.

Dominic threw his legs over the side of the bed and sat up. "What did it cost you?"

"Hell, boss," Dub said with relish. "You're spending too much money. I figured we should go back to our old methods, so I told him to give me the file or I'd break all his fingers."

Dominic smiled thinly. "Dub, I've asked you not to 'figure.' "

"I know you have, boss, but what you have here in me is not your ordinary errand boy. I've got a mind, see, and I got to use it, you might say, in spite of myself. It's active. It ticks right along. I always do what you tell me to, but

217

sometimes I ask myself, Why am I doing this? What does my boss want? How could I do it even better?"

Dub was going to go on to tell how he *had* broken all of Bradley's fingers, but Dominic said, "Disembarrass yourself of that notion, Dub. You do not have a mind, and you should not proceed as if you did."

"It's okay, boss, I'm not embarrassed." Dub smiled from ear to ear and rubbed his hands together, wanting to tell his story but beginning to suspect that his boss was trying to tell him he shouldn't be creative.

Dominic took a penknife from his pocket and cut the string that bound the bunch of manila envelopes together. The file was named Bartha and was divided into: Husbands, Children, Soo Yung, Tom, Joel, Fred, Miyami.

At first Dominic just gave it a cursory look. It was clear to him at once that this man Bradley was investigating Miliana, not the fire. Dominic was impressed, a feeling that was rare with him. If I'd had this man working for me, he thought, I'd have found Miliana within a month. The thought was extremely painful.

There was another knock at the door. Dub went to answer and returned with a tray. "I figured when you saw how big the file was, you'd want to take your lunch in here, so I ordered it up for you. Hot pastrami on onion roll. A beer and a cheesecake. Did I figure that one right?"

Dominic nodded in an absent-minded way, which Dub was able to take as an enormous vote of confidence in his abilities.

"Before you read the file, boss, just let me tell you how I see the big picture of what it is you want here: You want to find out from Bradley's records whether anyone else is after your wife, and if he is, we knock him off, right? Because now you want her to live. We spend six years looking for her so you can kill her. Now we spend the rest of our lives making sure no one else kills her. I gotta tell you I'm bewildered here."

"I sense an aggrieved tone, Dub. You have been only a minor foot soldier in a battalion of people looking for her, as you will be in our present search for the arsonist. You have a problem?"

"No, no!" Dub held up both hands placatingly. "It's okay. It's fine. It's a good idea to keep her out of harm's way is my feeling."

Dominic said gently, "I'm glad you approve. I see there's no way I can keep you from 'figuring.' Just don't vocalize it, okay? That means," he said, his gentle tone segueing into an ominous one, "shut up. You've never seen any 'picture' bigger than a postage stamp and you never will."

Dub grinned happily. "You know what? That's the most words you've said in a month. I think you're beginning to feel better and boy, am I glad. I've been worried about you, real worried. I'd like to take this moment now to say that you're a wonderful person and I love working for you, Mr. Racatelli."

Dominic reached into his bedside table and withdrew a gun with a silencer. "What's this?" he asked, pointing to the silencer.

Dub told him and, getting the message, stopped talking, only allowing himself to hum happily to himself as they started perusing the files together.

nine

The next morning, Tom and Miliana set out for a walk on the mountain. It was one of those soft, moist, not quite drizzly days that obscure the distance but enhance the colors of the near. It was warm but not warm enough for a Mexican dress, so Miliana donned a pair of pants, belting in the still slack waist, and pulled one of Tom's big hooded sweatshirts over her head.

They walked single file along the Sun Trail, Miliana exclaiming at all the spring wildflowers that had bloomed in her absence, poppies, lupines, iris, buttercups.

She kept falling back. Tom would stop and wait for her. At first he thought it was because she kept pausing to oh and ah over the flowers, but then he watched and realized she was moving terribly slowly. "If you keep taking two steps backward for every forward step, we won't make much progress," he joked.

"I'm sorry. I'm so used to going at a snail's pace in the Yucatán heat, I've forgotten how to stride out briskly. Why don't you go on at your own pace and I'll just dawdle. I'm having such fun drinking it all in. My beloved mountain. How I missed it." As he still stood there, she gave him a push. "Go on."

"But I want to walk with you."

"Nonsense, you need your exercise, and as you pointed out"—she laughed—"this isn't walking, it's almost standing still." Seeing he was going to be obstinate,

220

she glared at him. "I mean it, Tom. It will just upset me if I feel I'm holding you up, and then I won't enjoy myself."

"Okay. Will you be home when I get back?"

"Yes. I'm supposed to go see Miyami today, but I think I'll put it off. I want to see Joel and Soo Yung, since I haven't greeted either of them yet. But mostly I want to spend the day with you."

They hugged and kissed, then she watched him disappear along the trail into the mist. She sat down in the welter of orange poppies, then she lay back in them, looking up at the sky. She could see blue beyond the veil. I'm so happy, she thought. This is it, Mother Goose: lying in poppies, swathed in mountain mist, the blue beyond, Tom striding manfully away so as to return to me soon. What a lucky woman I am. What a good life it's been. But I think I'm at the end of my strength.

"Three wise men of Gotham / Went to sea in a bowl. / And if the bowl had been stronger / My song had been longer."

Her increasingly wet clothes roused her from her epiphany, so she rose to her feet, pushing off with her hands, and started back. When she got in view of her house, she saw Joel's truck and then Joel. She hailed him and, although still moving slowly, hastened to him in her heart. He came to meet her, giving her a big hug. "Welcome home, Max!"

"Thank you! It's great to be back. I've called you a couple of times but no luck. The bedroom's perfectly beautiful. Beyond my wildest dreams."

"It ought to be; it cost me a bundle."

"Which is only my due," she reminded him. "Or, as you would say, my fucking due."

He laughed. They went into the house.

"Heat up the coffee while I get some dry clothes." She put on a Mexican dress, the one with lavender and coral flowers embroidered at neck and hem, and belted it in with a pink sash.

"Oh, that's nice," he said when she appeared. "You look wonderful, Max. Different somehow, but good. Real good. When do we get to christen the bedroom?"

"Well," she said, pouring out two mugs of coffee and sitting down on the couch before the view, "this is a surprise invitation!"

As usual, Joel didn't sit. "I've missed you," he said, then went on to surprise her even more. "I want to be with you. In fact, I want to marry you."

Miliana's jaw fell. Joel laughed to see it. He sat down beside her and embraced her. "I mean it. I want to spend the rest of my life with you, if you'll have me."

She kissed him warmly back, then said, "Joel, you don't want to get married. You never have. And if ever you do, you'll want a young woman who can give you some kids and look after you in your declining years—which are starting pretty soon, by the way."

"There's plenty of good meals to be got off an old stove," he said.

That was one of Tom's favorite lines too.

Miliana was amazed. She knew Joel had never in his life asked someone to marry him. Then she remembered the "betrayal," which had actually left her mind for a while, and it seemed to her that the only possible reason Joel could have for asking her to marry him was guilt. It was the only way to make up to her for selling her out to Dominic.

"Oh, Joel, was it you?" Tears sprang to her eyes.

"Was who me?"

"Judas."

"Iscariot?" Joel had been raised a Catholic and, unlike Tom, was well versed in his Bible. Thank goodness. Miliana couldn't have borne it if Joel mused aloud about an Iscariot among his acquaintances in the construction trade, perhaps one of the obscure sheet metalists or tapers, many of whom had funny names.

"One of you betrayed me to Dominic," she said. She had almost said, "Verily, verily I say unto you that one of you," etc. Already, the terrible business of the betrayal was losing its thrust. Now that she was home, on her dear mountain, among her loved ones, the Dominic business seemed like a dream, and the betrayal something not to be taken seriously, being too fantastic and biblical. Did it matter, really? After all, she was alive, wasn't she?

It must have mattered, because she went on with it. Joel was back on his feet now, wandering around the room, so that she had to keep turning her head as she spoke. "You or Tom or Soo Yung actually accepted money to tell Dominic I was in Uxmal."

Joel seemed unimpressed and only said, "I wonder if it would have covered my building costs. By the way, I'm going to give you a bill for fifty thousand, which should get you enough insurance money to cover your medical."

"Thank you. That's wonderful. I won't have to sell the house. But you don't seem in the least disturbed by my news. Or else you're just avoiding the subject, trying to wriggle away."

"You're the one wriggling away from my marriage proposal."

"It is your proposal that leads me to think you are the Judas. You want to marry me only to make up for your betrayal."

"If you think that, then to hell with you!"

"Well, I don't really think it, because I don't see that marriage to you would be any kind of compensation. It would be hell. Every time I opened the trailer door there'd be a woman in there, and the rest of the time you'd be working night and day."

"Which reminds me, Max—that woman you scared the shit out of has gone back to New Zealand."

"New Zealand? Joel! Bradley's from New Zealand. The Polynesian Investigator. And he told me he originally came here to visit his sister. It could be a coincidence. There could be multitudes of New Zealanders around. But they're the only two *I* ever met. Joel, remember when we had dinner in Tiburon? Wasn't she the woman who stared at us from across the room?"

"Right, and the blond man she was with was Bradley."

"And we were followed from the restaurant. Cleverly followed, as an investigator would know how to do. So he learned that night where my house was. What if that girl simply said to him, Find out about that woman Joel is with. Then he set the fire so that under the aegis of investigating it, he could investigate me."

Miliana went on to tell Joel what Seez had said about seeing the blond man before the fire. "He probably didn't mean to hurt me, since the house was empty at the time. But it allowed him to look into my life officially. Then his sister, learning I was burned and probably knowing her brother had set the fire, got scared and left, feeling it was her fault. I bet now that he's seen Seez, Bradley's making like a homing pigeon too."

"He better be, or he's going to be pounded to a pulp. That little prick."

"It's funny how one often does want to know about one's rival," Miliana mused. "It becomes obsessively fascinating to know every tiny thing as if you were married to her through the man you both love."

"Does that make me married to Tom?"

"Absolutely."

"Speaking of marriage . . ."

"Let's speak about the betrayal first."

"Max, if you think for one minute I sold you out I don't want to marry you."

She could tell that he meant it. "I did think about it and for more than a minute."

"Then I'm out of the proposal with my honor intact."

Miliana smiled. "I do love you, you know."

"But not enough to marry me."

"I am still married to Dominic. I could divorce him but I think I'd do better to let sleeping dogs lie."

"It's the fireman. I think you love Tom more than me. I just don't get it." Joel looked pained.

Miliana realized that since he hadn't proposed out of guilt, it must truly have been from love, and she hadn't responded graciously. "Joel." She stood up and put a hand against his cheek. "I'm so honored that you asked me to be your wife." Verily verily I am, she thought. "You are a good man, one in a million. All I want is your happiness and I know I would not make you happy. Please don't be angry. Please don't want to kill me."

He took her hand from his cheek and kissed it in a gesture so touching, tears filled her eyes.

"I always want to kill you, Max," he said. "But first I'm going to kill Bradley." He grabbed his jacket. "Thanks for the coffee."

"Thanks for being the best friend in the world."

She walked out with him and waved him away. She felt sad, as if she would not see him again. She had the feeling she should have said more to him, some last good words to go on with, like: Slow down, take it easy, don't work and love at such a killing pace. But this is silly, she thought. I'll see him again. Won't I?

Tom arrived back from his hike. "Did I see Joel's truck go by?"

"Yes." She started to tell him the latest on Bradley, but it began to seem so wearying, so complicated, so boring, such past history. What did it matter? What mattered was now.

Tom seemed to be waiting for something. She just said, "Joel and I had a nice visit. It was good to see him."

"Why do you look so sad?"

"I don't know. An hour ago, lying in the spring flowers, I felt so happy I could have died. But then I felt chilled. It's funny that you can feel happy enough to die but not enough to get chilled."

ten

Dominic and Dub had finished their lunch and were still looking over Bradley's files. Dominic was up to "Miyami," Dub was on "Fred."

Dominic, upon opening the Miyami file, was thinking Bradley had to be incredibly resourceful to have got hold of medical records, which even the patient never sees. But by now he understood the obsessive curiosity of the man. He was simply unable to stop. As long as there was something more to know, some thread to follow, he continued relentlessly.

Dominic idly scanned the doctor's cryptic notations, as he mused about Bradley. Suddenly a tremor went through him, causing the papers to rustle. He closed the file, stood up, and went to the window, his back to Dub.

"Hey, boss, what does this mean, 'the little blighter'?"

Dominic was quiet, then, his voice strained, he said, "He's referring to the dog."

"I know that, but what does 'little blighter' mean? I want to know. I like to increase my vocabulary is why."

"It is British slang for a no-account person, or, in this case, dog. I don't think it would be appropriate for you to make it a part of your repertoire. It would only confuse your listeners . . . even more."

Dub laid down the file and looked terribly pleased. "I think I've figured the whole thing out. The way I see it is, this guy Caesar could have tried to kill your wife because he thought she'd taken his dog. If you ask me, this Caesar isn't playing with a full deck neither."

"I think you are in a good position to discern that, Dub."

" 'Discern' isn't in my vocabulary yet either, but never mind that. What do you think? Is Seez our man or ain't he? Do I blow him away?"

Dominic whipped around, his body stiff with anger. "No, he is not. And no, you do not. You have never blown anything but your nose and my instructions." His eyes flared, his nostrils seemed to emit steam.

Dub stood and backed himself up to the wall. "Jeez, boss, I didn't mean nothing."

"Again, I ask you to give up your fantasies and your speculations," Dominic said chillingly. "You are essentially my valet and my chauffeur, both of which you do well. Also, you are outstandingly good-natured, which I appreciate." His anger departed as fast as it had come. He went on talking as if from a memorized speech, no longer caring, just finishing to get it over. "However, Dub, when I ask you to do a little something extra by way of an errand, it goes to your head in the most astonishing way. Why?" he said distractedly. "Why?"

"It's because I want to get on in the organization, boss," Dub explained, wondering if now was the time to relate his finger-breaking technique.

Dominic sighed, went to the mirror, and tightened his tie. He put on his jacket. "Anyhow, it doesn't matter anymore, Dub. What we're looking for . . . isn't a guy."

Dub, too, made ready for departure. "Where are we going?"

"Relax. I'm going to see Dr. Miyami. I'll drive myself.

Take the afternoon off. I'll be needing you this evening at seven."

While Dominic was crossing the bridge to Marin County, Miliana was driving north to Sonoma County, to Soo Yung's little cottage by the fruit tree. She had called her to say that she would arrive in the early afternoon, and Soo Yung had sounded delighted. Although it was Monday, she explained that she had the day off because she worked through the weekends, the busiest time for tours.

When Soo Yung opened her door, she was struck by how beautiful Miliana looked. Her beauty was different, not as fabulous as before but more subtle, almost unearthly.

She gave her a warm hug and kiss and exclaimed, "How well you look! Joel and Tom must be vying for your attentions like crazy."

"But, Soo Yung, *you* look perfectly marvelous. Is this you? In jeans and boots, and your hair all cropped like a boy? You look so dashing, so alive. You must have lost your religion. I'm so glad! And what a sweet place."

"Isn't it adorable? See how light it is! What a difference light makes."

"No piano," said Miliana.

"Right. And no lessons. Instead a first-rate stereo. I shall never make music again: I will listen to it. Plus, the Santa Rosa Symphony is terrific. Come, sit down. I've made you some coffee. Or you can have a glass of Chardonnay if you like."

"I do like."

While Soo Yung went to the kitchen, Miliana sat

down on the couch. She was sincerely happy for her friend. Soo Yung is going to be all right, she thought, with relief and pleasure. Seeing her so happy brought home to her how depressed she must have been before. The little house was charming, the furniture, rugs, curtains, all attractive and colorful and, she couldn't help but notice, brand new.

Hmmm.

Of course, this job could pay handsomely, but . . . the price of the stereo alone! And hadn't she seen a new yellow Honda out front? Hmmm.

But would Soo Yung be so blatant? Well, yes, she would, if she hadn't expected Miliana to return. But she had returned, was here now, and Soo Yung did not seem the least abashed, let alone stricken with guilt. Why, those boots alone, thought Miliana, accepting the wine from Soo Yung's hand, are three-hundred-dollar items or I'll eat my hat. This is all beginning to look pretty detestable.

All her good feeling at seeing her friend again, and finding her so happy, began to drain away. She fixed her with a baleful eye.

"Miliana, what's come over you? If looks could kill."

Miliana stood up. Too suddenly. It made her dizzy. She sat down again and took a sip of the wine.

"Are you all right?"

"I feel like puking."

Now Soo Yung stood up as if to run for a bowl. "Never mind." Miliana stopped her. "It's just a figure of speech," she said, although it wasn't entirely. "I'm not really going to puke. I just feel like it. It will pass."

"Well," said Soo Yung, cozying into an armchair, her legs tucked under her. "Tell me about Dominic."

230

"What?"

"Didn't he find you? I told him you were at Uxmal. How do you think I got all this money?" She spread her arms, displaying the treasures of her light-filled quarters.

Miliana's jaw fell for the second time that day. Again she felt faint. "Soo Yung, I just don't understand how you can blithely tell me that. And I certainly don't understand how you, my best and oldest friend, could have sold me out."

"Oh, Miliana." Soo Yung affected great weariness. "I beg of you not to dramatize this thing any longer."

"You betrayed me," Miliana said hotly, wishing she could rise to her feet and express herself with more body movement so that this dread confrontation wouldn't look like such a cozy womanly chat. "You made it possible for Dominic to find me and kill me. And all for gain."

"Oh, I'm sorry," Soo Yung said sarcastically. "I didn't notice that you were dead."

Miliana flushed. "It is only due to my own resourcefulness that I am not."

"Oh, yes." Soo Yung laughed. "And I'm sure you have some exciting tale to tell me. A chase scene, no doubt. At night. Up and down countless pyramids. Come on, tell me—I really do want to hear. Except that I'd like to hear the *real* story."

Miliana's incapacitating astonishment, anger, and embarrassment began to retreat as she got a glimmer of what was going on. "You never did believe that Dominic wanted to kill me? All this time?"

"Of course not. But I humored you. I believed that you believed it. I also believed—in fact, I *knew*—that he was pursuing you all these years. What I can't understand is that you still, even now, even after seeing him, think that he was after you to kill you, rather than to get you back. Dominic loves you."

"Dominic hates me so much you wouldn't believe it," Miliana said furiously, talking through a clenched jaw the way Tom did when he was pretending to be tough, only her face had truly gone into a spasm. "Dominic's hatred for me is absolutely monumental. In fact, there should be a monument to it, not an equestrian statue but something along the lines of the Eiffel Tower or the Library of Congress. You have just persuaded yourself differently so you can live with this hideous betrayal and so you can spend your blood money with abandon."

"Just explain to me why you are alive, then," Soo Yung exclaimed, getting exercised herself, uncurling her legs and sitting bolt upright. "I would say that your presence here is self-evident. I never thought for one second that you would not return from Uxmal. Dominic would never lay a finger on you. He would kill himself first. I don't understand how you inspire such love in people, Miliana," she said almost bitterly, her old resentment returning in spite of her glorious light-filled, money-laden new life. "But you do."

Miliana drained her glass and set it down. "You have fallen as low as a person can fall. The tragedy is that you don't even realize it. I can only hope that your unconscious mind will eventually apprise you of your foul deed and you will begin, like Lady Macbeth, to constantly wash your hands or, even better, your boots."

With this, Miliana at last found the strength to get to her feet and leave. More accurately, she found the will to pretend that her body had the strength to rise to its feet and go out the door.

"You will see that I am right, Miliana," Soo Yung

shouted after her, rather hysterically, "and then you will apologize to me for these cruel words. What's more," she screamed, "you have never stopped loving Dominic yourself."

Miliana drove rapidly home. She didn't feel very well and thought it would be nice to lie down. In fact, she felt awful. In the Yucatán, she had been able to convince herself that she was getting stronger, but now, back on her old stomping ground, where she could compare her present self to her former, she saw that she was only a shadow. What's more, she suspected it hadn't to do with her burns, for she remembered that her physical strength had begun to diminish before the fire. She supposed Dr. Miyami, when she saw him tomorrow, would be able to tell her what was the matter. She wasn't at all sure that she wanted to know.

Meanwhile Dr. Miyami was telling Dominic, who had introduced himself as Miliana's husband, what was the matter with her, corroborating what Dominic had learned from her stolen charts.

"Yes," the doctor said. "Your wife has leukemia. When I felt she was sufficiently recovered from her operations, I was going to put her in the hands of an oncologist for chemotherapy, but for some reason unknown to me, she left the hospital on her own and nobody was able to tell me where she had gone. Naturally I have been very anxious. She is home now and was to have come in today, but she put the appointment off until tomorrow."

"She doesn't know?"

"No. Recovering from her burns, she was in no condition to be told."

"How long does she have?"

Miyami said vaguely, "I don't know how much further the disease has progressed."

Dominic stood up and came over to his desk, leaning on it with his hands. He looked deeply into Miyami's eyes. "How long does she have?" he asked again.

Miyami had seen all kinds of pain in his life. This was something else. "I'm surprised she's still alive," he said.

eleven

The title of Miliana's last essay was "To Live Like Mother Goose." It was only a page and a half long and this is what it said:

Okay, this is it, children, and world, the definitive rhyme! Are you ready?

> Jog on, jog on, the footpath way
> And merrily jump the stile, boys.
> A merry heart goes all the way—
> Your sad one tires in a mile, boys.

What is there to add to this? Nothing. It is perfect. Those four little lines tell you how to live. As does Mother Goose in her own person.

I realize that all along I've pictured Mother Goose as a goose. In her appearances to me, or in the sounds that betokened her presence—fluttering wings, etc.—she was, manifestly, a goose. But in her mortal life, she was a person, probably a woman.

She made no sense, made nonsense, made good sense. Her senses were keen. She was fantastically alive. Live like her if you can—merrily. All the way.

Be simple, imaginative, sensitive, and funny. Scorn selfishness, whininess, cowardice, and greed. Be a man and, what is harder, be a woman.

Be flexible. Love animals. And each other. Adam, look out for your sisters. All three of you, be there for each other and for your friends. But don't clutter up your life with a lot of people who aren't important to you. Three children, one husband, two lovers, and a woman friend is perfect.

Take long walks, watch sunsets.

A little excitement in life is good, but one can overdo.

Stay alert. Learn to play the piano. Lose your temper, when pressed, but be quick to say you're sorry. Keep the house clean, hang up your clothes and—what else? Oh, yes—always remember how much your mother loves you and how proud she is of you, my darling children, and world.

Miliana added these pages to her legacy pile, stood up, and stretched. It had been a long day and life.

It was eight o'clock, and the setting sun was only just beginning to color the sky. Tom was out on the deck in the hot tub, having a good soak. His back was to her as he looked toward the lemon-colored sunset. The room was dark, but she decided not to put on the lamps. Instead she went to the piano and sat down. As always, she heard Dominic's voice instructing her. *All the great innovators and creators in jazz, the leading edge that captures everyone's imagination, all the great stylists that everyone flips out over, have always been black. It's a fact of our universe. No one knows why exactly. But we don't have to understand why, do we? We can just be grateful.*

The only thing I'd do different if I could do it all again, thought Miliana, is be black instead of an Argentinian Jew, and be a composer. I've had a lot of fun, but it would have been nice to contribute one nice song and leave that for a legacy instead of my idiotic essays.

She remembered Dizzy Gillespie, talking about his composition "Night in Tunisia," how it had started out as simply a nice song and had somehow, over the years, "moseyed into the metaphysical."

She smiled and began to play another song of his, called "Things to Come." Out in the hot tub, Tom raised his hand and gave the thumbs-up sign.

"That's good, Miliana. It swings." Dominic's voice again.

She was pleased with his praise.

It took her a full minute to realize that this time his voice was not in her mind.

Her heart pounding, Miliana turned and saw him standing in the shadows just inside the door. She wanted to greet him in some perfect way to show how cool she was, but no words came. She eased her legs over to the other side of the piano bench so she could face him. What was it she'd said to the menace in the salon during the cornered-rat incident? "It's you, is it? What a surprise." That was pretty good, but she did not want Dominic to think she was surprised. Anyhow, she wasn't surprised. "I've been waiting for you," were his first words after the six-year interval. Not appropriate here. Except she realized that she *had* been waiting for him.

He spoke again. "And, yes," he said. "Since you ask, I still do play."

"It took you a while to answer. Was there anything else?"

"This." He raised the gun.

A light came to her eye. "I see. You found out I pulled a fast one and now you've come to finish me off."

For some reason, Miliana felt as if an electric current

had switched on in her. It lit up her eyes and charged her body with energy. She felt fully alive.

He didn't answer.

"You thought I was old and decrepit and then you found out I was better than ever. Probably from Soo Yung, that Judas. I hope, after you shoot me, she'll go and hang herself and keep up the tradition thereby. It would be awful if, because of her, future Judases of the world just went on spending sprees."

"You look extremely beautiful right now."

"I foxed you." She couldn't seem to stop bragging. Maybe she wanted to impress him that somehow, no matter what, she was still the winner. Of what, she wasn't sure. Her body was all strung up, as if poised for flight. She was glad that Dominic could see her like this and not remember her as all wobbly and witless. "I could still call out for Tom," she said.

"Yes, but there wouldn't be time enough."

"He's thick of hearing anyhow. But do me one favor, Dominic. Remove the silencer so he'll hear the shot and come to me. I'll want to say goodbye. He's been such a good friend. Shoot me in such a way that I'll have one last minute."

Miliana relaxed her body and shifted her weight so she leaned on one arm, her head resting on her shoulder. "I'm not scared." One last brag.

"I know. Goodbye, Max."

"Goodbye, Dominic."

Tom did hear the shot. He catapulted out of the tub and raced into the house. Miliana was on the floor, bleeding. She raised her arms to him. Professional rescuer, he immediately stanched the blood with his towel and, holding her to his breast, reached for the phone.

"No, Tom, there isn't time. Can you hear me? I love you."

Tom began to cry. The tears coursed down his face. "You're okay," he said, even though he knew it was arterial blood soaking the towel.

"It's a good way to go. This is exactly how I wanted it." She smiled tremulously. "Tom?"

"What, Max?"

She was looking over his shoulder now, the light fading from her eyes, still smiling. "I see him coming for me . . . all bent and twisted . . . so all along the crooked man . . . was death. I led him a merry chase, didn't I? All the way."

Dub was waiting with the motor going. Dominic stepped quickly into the back seat. Dub looked around at him, concerned. "You okay, boss? You don't look too good."

Dominic did not reply, only gestured for him to drive on. Dub put the car in gear and sped away into the night.

Dominic put the silencer back on the gun. He pressed the muzzle into his mouth so he would die instantly. No last minutes for him, no other goodbye. He smiled a little, thinking of the conversation with his wife. I'm not scared either, Max, he thought. That was his last thought.